I0536337

THE RETIREMENT MURDERS

Esther & Jack Enright Mystery
Book Nine

David Field

SAPERE
BOOKS

THE
RETIREMENT
MURDERS

Published by Sapere Books.

24 Trafalgar Road, Ilkley, LS29 8HH

saperebooks.com

Copyright © David Field, 2025

David Field has asserted his right to be identified as the author of this work.
All rights reserved.

No part of this publication may be reproduced, stored in any retrieval system, or transmitted, in any form, or by any means, electronic, mechanical, photocopying, recording, or otherwise, without the prior written permission of the publishers.
This book is a work of fiction. Names, characters, businesses, organisations, places and events, other than those clearly in the public domain, are either the product of the author's imagination, or are used fictitiously.
Any resemblances to actual persons, living or dead, events or locales are purely coincidental.

ISBN: 978-0-85495-653-1

CHAPTER ONE

Essex, 1898

Esther Enright tutted loudly as she brushed some dandruff from the uniform jacket being worn by her husband Jack as he stood in front of her. 'You shouldn't wash your hair with the same soap that you use in the bath,' she admonished him. 'That's why I leave that oil on the side — how many times do I have to remind you?'

'Do stop fussing,' Jack protested. 'It's bad enough that I have to wear this damned uniform on special occasions, because the serge is scratchy where it meets the skin. Most days, I can get away with wearing an ordinary civilian suit.'

'Today isn't "most days", though, is it?' Esther pointed out. 'Today you get to say goodbye to the uncle who talked you into joining the police force in the first place. Your mother never quite forgave him, and now that she's gone I regard it as my sworn duty to mark the occasion by saying "Good riddance to a bad influence".'

'I won't exactly be saying goodbye to him,' Jack said. 'He just won't be alongside me in the Met, that's all.'

'Well, let's be grateful for small mercies, anyway,' Esther replied with a frown. 'That last exploit nearly got the pair of you killed. But at least it invalided Percy out of the force, where he can't get you into any more life-threatening escapades.'

'I'll tell him that you send your best regards on his compulsory retirement,' Jack said with a smile. 'Now, have you finished inspecting me for nits?'

'That wasn't what I was doing,' said Esther curtly, 'but you're free to go. Don't let Percy lead you astray on his final day.'

'Not even Uncle Percy could do that during a farewell party,' Jack said.

Esther's eyebrows shot up. 'He got you both shot at when you were supposed to be investigating a straightforward stolen property case, so I'm not convinced. It may well have been a deliberate ploy on his part to get himself out of the force on a full pension, but I can only thank a merciful Providence that you weren't the one who got wounded.'

'It wasn't deliberate, trust me,' Jack said with a grimace as he was reminded of the nerve-racking time he'd spent under a wagon in a pub yard in Plaistow, trying to staunch the bullet wound in Percy's shoulder while fighting off a group of determined gun smugglers who they'd tracked down.

They'd both come out of it alive, feted as heroes by the more sensationalist of the daily newspapers, and each had received their own reward. For Percy, now fully recovered, it had been a somewhat 'creative' medical opinion regarding his likely return date to active service. It coincided with his scheduled retirement date, and now he was about to leave the career with which he'd recently become disenchanted a year early, on full pension. Today was the day of his retirement party, which was to take place at the Scotland Yard headquarters. Jack had been invited to join all the other former colleagues who'd be enjoying a few glasses of beer, along with pork pies and sausage rolls, at the ceremony organised by Chief Superintendent Herbert Montague, Percy and Jack's superior officer.

Jack's reward had been designed as much for the benefit of the Met as for Jack, although it was nevertheless something of a major honour for a man still only in his thirty-second year. A new rank had been created for his benefit, that of Chief Inspector, sitting in the Met hierarchy between the ranks of Inspector and Superintendent, and denoted by the rows of shiny pips on each shoulder of his uniform jacket. This new rank had been created in order to dignify the equally new Recruitment and Manpower Branch within the Met that Jack was the head of, in the hope that his own background as a middle-class, grammar school-educated young man would encourage others like himself to follow his example and become heroes in uniform.

'Why's Daddy got his uniform on?' Esther and Jack's older son Bertie asked. Even at the age of five he was fascinated by uniforms, in particular military ones such as those painted on his toy soldiers.

'Because he needs to look smart, and it fits him perfectly,' replied his older sister, six-year-old Lily, who hadn't been the one asked, but whose lifelong rivalry with Bertie guaranteed that she'd be the one with the superior rejoinder as they lurked in the open doorway to the living room. Behind them stood their siblings, Miriam, aged two, and Tommy, who had just started to walk.

'It perhaps needed a little more across the shoulders,' Esther told her, proud to share with their oldest child the tailoring skills that she'd learned during her unmarried days as a seamstress in the East End. Lily was as fascinated with fashion and needlework as Bertie was with toy soldiers.

'It'll need a little more across the waist, if I emulate Uncle Percy's interest in food,' Jack grimaced. 'I only hope that the caterers we hired do him proud. Anyway, time for me to leave, if I'm to catch the nine-twenty.'

It was a brisk twenty-minute walk from the house in Church Lane that the family had inherited from Jack's mother to the station in the centre of Barking. There Jack was able to employ the first-class rail pass that came with his rank in order to rattle his way down to Fenchurch Street on the non-stop nine-twenty service maintained by the London, Tilbury and Southend Railway. He then had a choice between a horse bus, again courtesy of a free pass, or a private cab — an occasional luxury that he allowed himself today — in order to complete the journey across north-east London to his place of employment in Victoria.

Once installed in his third-floor office, and with several hours to fill before Uncle Percy's send-off scheduled for three that afternoon, Jack reached into his in-tray for the latest list of applications from those who were hoping to enter the Metropolitan Police service at constable level. The ones that had made it to this stage had passed through the various filters designed to eliminate those who failed to satisfy the very basic requirements. Jack's current practice was to interview them all, although if recruitment levels rose any higher he'd need to delegate some of the work.

Applicants had to be aged between twenty-one and twenty-seven, stand at least five feet nine inches tall in bare feet, be able to read and write, possess what was described as 'general' intelligence, and be free from any 'bodily complaint'. These qualifications had become more exacting over the years; those who'd been recruited in Jack's day had only needed to be over the age of eighteen. Jack himself had turned eighteen only two days before he'd finally realised the ambition inspired in him by Uncle Percy, himself a serving officer at the time. He'd been a surrogate father to Jack, who had lodged with Percy and his wife, Aunt Beatrice, after his father had died when Jack had been fourteen years old.

Jack ate only a brief meal in the Senior Officers' Dining Room, conscious of the fact that there would be food available at the farewell party, which would be held in this very same room once it had been cleared of regular customers. He then went for a stroll down Victoria Embankment to make room for whatever culinary delights would be available when Percy took his final bow.

Two hours later, Jack wandered back into the bustling room. It seemed to be full of high-ranking officers, all in their dress uniforms, while Percy, predictably, had ignored protocol and was wearing the same suit that he normally wore to church. Jack's Aunt Beattie dragged Percy to the early Sunday service whenever he couldn't claim to be required at work.

'Esther sends her warm regards, and still insists that you're a bad influence,' Jack said as he sidled up to where Percy had set up camp alongside the beer barrel, and reached out for a sausage roll from the trestle table draped in white. He smiled graciously at the young lady in a black dress, white apron and matching cap who was standing next to it, advising those attending what could be found inside the sandwiches and pastries.

'She's probably right,' Percy said as he raised his beer glass in a silent salute, 'but from today you'll have to find some other excuse. How is she, by the way? The usual river of wifely chastisement?'

'She hasn't changed in that way,' Jack admitted, 'but I wouldn't want her to stop, because then I'd worry that she didn't care about me anymore. She's still enjoying teaching at the local school, even though Bertie and Lily are no longer in her class, and she's not required to prise them apart when they wage war on each other. And before you ask, Miriam is a delight as ever, while Tommy's now walking like a drunken navvy on pay night. With all that to manage, you'd expect Esther to go more lightly on me, but no chance.'

'If wifely criticism is a reliable judge,' said Percy, chuckling, 'then your Aunt Beattie adores me to the point of distraction.'

'I still can't quite bring myself to believe that you agreed to go a year early,' Jack replied, 'given her cooking, and her determination to find tasks to occupy your every waking minute.'

'That's why I find the garden so attractive,' Percy said. 'I actually hate gardening, but your aunt suffers from hay fever, so once I cross the rear lawn and disappear behind the runner bean trellises I might as well be in India. But I really *was* brassed off with the job, Jack. That business with the murdered babies made me finally realise that policing is all about maintaining the status quo between the social classes — making sure that the "have nots" don't get their hands on the stuff owned by the "haves".'

'At least the force will be spared the sound of you on your Socialist soapbox,' said a stentorian voice to Jack's left. He almost dropped his beer glass as he recognised it, and turned to smile with what he hoped looked like enthusiasm at Chief Superintendent Montague, resplendent in his braid, pips and army medals. Jack made polite excuses as he slipped away, armed with a sausage roll and a refill for his beer glass. He found a quiet corner where he could observe the proceedings without having to contribute to them.

Percy forced a smile to his lips as he turned to address Montague. 'Thank you for organising this little gathering,' he said, 'if only to make sure that I'm actually going to be leaving the building for the final time.'

'It was the least I could do for an officer with your track record, Percy,' Montague replied, 'and at least after today we can expect crimes to be investigated in accordance with the Procedures Manual. And we can hope that suspects will actually come to trial alive.'

'Those were unfortunate accidents,' Percy protested mildly with a giveaway twinkle in his eye. 'And I believe I still hold the Yard record for the number of closed case files.'

'I shall be making reference to those in my little speech,' said Montague. 'Along with a few anecdotes supplied to me by those you worked closely with.'

'My nephew cannot necessarily be relied upon not to gild the lily,' Percy warned him. 'When he was lodging with my wife and myself, and lost some item or other such as his school satchel or a football, the loss was always attributed to it having been wrenched from his steely grip by a marauding squad of urban terrorists. In reality, he had a habit of leaving things on park benches.'

'Be that as it may, I hope that you'll find what I have to say about you both fair and acceptable. Is this beer drinkable, by the way? The caterers were suspiciously cheap, and one or two of those sandwiches look a little tired already.'

'I had a pork pie,' Percy said, 'but it did taste a bit off.'

'How's that nephew of yours coping with his new responsibilities?' Montague asked as he poured himself a generous measure of beer from the tap protruding from the cask.

'We haven't had much occasion to discuss them,' Percy replied diplomatically, 'but knowing Jack, he'll make the best fist of it that he can. He certainly has the benefit of a supportive wife and a secure home life, and he was very grateful that, as a non-operational officer, he could continue to reside in the old family home in Barking.'

'Jolly good,' Montague replied. Seemingly having assessed that he'd spent the appropriate amount of time exchanging pleasantries with Percy, he moved towards Assistant Commissioner Bruce who was hovering in the doorway, no doubt seeking some officer of appropriate rank to escort him into the proceedings.

A further half hour ensued, which Jack filled by watching the comings and goings, having rarely seen so many high-ranking men in the same room. Once it began to look as if all the invitees had arrived, several waitresses in their black and white service uniforms began circulating with trays of canapés containing delicacies such as smoked salmon, oysters and curried egg. Once these had been consumed, fruit tarts and cream cakes were brought in and left on the centre table.

Percy was still in his original position, within an enthusiast's reach of the beer cask, when Montague walked back over and instructed, 'Put down that drink for a moment, Percy, and join me over in the corner if you will. They've set up a lectern that I can use while extolling your virtues.'

Both men put down their beer glasses and walked over to the rostrum that had been retrieved from the Yard's copious storeroom. Someone called for silence, and a hush fell over the room as Montague raised his voice.

'I was invited here today to deliver a eulogy for one of the most admired officers that the Met has ever known. A man whose devotion to duty, adherence to the Procedure Manuals, respect for authority and obedience to orders from senior officers has made him a legend within the police service. Instead, I find myself talking about Detective Chief Inspector Percy Enright.'

The laughter was loud and protracted. Even Percy had a grin on his face as he raised his hand in silent acknowledgement of the justice of the opening remark. Then Montague's tone softened as he continued.

'Working with Percy over the years has been an experience. For some, it has been a pleasant one, but fools, promotion-seekers and time-wasters soon learned to avoid him at all costs. He will be retiring as the officer in charge of the Discipline Branch, and no-one could have been better chosen to identify and smoke out the rule-breakers, given that no-one has broken more rules during his service career than Percy Enright.'

There were more appreciative chuckles, but Montague hadn't finished.

'I was chatting to Percy a few moments ago, and he reminded me of his unparalleled record for bringing in offenders — some of them actually still alive. It cannot be denied that there was no-one like Percy Enright when it came to sniffing out criminals, deviants and threats to this society of ours, particularly if they enjoyed what some would call "class privilege". Percy thought of this as an automatic indication of guilt.'

For the first time since beginning his speech, Montague consulted his notes.

'Percy began his career in Hackney, where he soon began to demonstrate his superior bargaining skills with the aid of a billy club. When the number of cracked heads among those brought into custody reached a concerning level, he was transferred to Bethnal Green, where his particular brand of law enforcement was better appreciated. He was then transferred to the Detective Branch here at the Yard, where he became one of a very large team that finally put an end to the career of the one they called "Jack the Ripper". In the process, he worked for the first time alongside his nephew Jack, who is with us here today, and so far as we have been able to ascertain has not inherited his uncle's affliction when it comes to following correct procedures. Together they proved to be a most effective team, until Percy elected to take on a gun-smuggling gang armed only with his own revolver, and a nephew who bravely preserved his life when Percy came second in a shooting contest. As a result of the injury he sustained on that occasion, Percy leaves us a year earlier than he might otherwise have done, and some twenty years *after* certain notable London criminals wished he had.'

Montague then gave a small hand signal, and two of Percy's former colleagues, now much higher in rank than he on his retirement, stepped forward carrying between them an ornate carriage clock.

'It's customary for those who've been most closely associated with a retiring officer to club together and present the retiree with a farewell gift to remind him of his career. As you can see, it's a carriage clock, and we have it on good authority that it does not feature on any of our stolen property lists. We cast the net widely when seeking contributions for this gift, but perhaps not surprisingly the amount collected from those of Percy's previous acquaintance now residing in Pentonville and Wandsworth proved to be disappointing. It just goes to show that there's no gratitude to be had from those of your former professional acquaintance.

'I asked around for any ideas regarding what Percy will do with all the free days that he now has ahead of him, and his nephew Jack suggested that the answer to that might be found in his vegetable garden. Therefore, we can confidently look forward to well arrested runner beans, sternly interrogated cabbages and rightly convicted carrots. And so I give you Percy Enright — all I ask is that you don't bring him back.'

There was a polite smattering of applause as Percy collected first his carriage clock, then his beer, and wandered across to where Jack was standing with a broad grin on his face.

'I've heard more complimentary farewell addresses,' he grumbled.

'But none as accurate, I would guess,' Jack replied.

'Less cheek from you to your uncle,' Percy demanded, but for once Jack was ready with the jibe that he'd been saving up all afternoon.

'It was a considered response from a higher ranking officer,' he said.

Percy nodded in acknowledgement, then looked down at the carriage clock. 'The last one of these we contemplated was indeed stolen, just before I helped you solve the riddle of those missing cargoes at Tilbury.'

'And I helped you locate those missing schoolboys, then net a group of gun smugglers, nearly getting myself killed in the process.'

'I already thanked you for saving my life — several times — so don't milk it,' Percy growled, just as a disturbance on the far side of the room grabbed their attention. There were several high-ranking colleagues surrounding Chief Superintendent Montague, two of them holding him upright by the arms. They gave up the struggle as his considerable weight took him from their grasp and he slid to the floor.

'I *did* warn him about those pork pies,' Percy muttered as he rushed over to where Montague was lying, a thick milky liquid oozing from his blue-tinged lips.

CHAPTER TWO

Assistant Commissioner Bruce called for the doors to the room to be locked, and for everyone inside to remain until they had all supplied statements, although it was not immediately obvious to whom those statements were to be given.

By happy coincidence, an urgent enquiry revealed that police surgeon Edward Galbraith was in the building delivering a report. He was hastily escorted to the Senior Officers' Dining Room, where he found Percy kneeling by the body of Chief Superintendent Montague, with his fingers on the side of his neck where his collar had been loosened.

'I think you'll find he's dead,' Percy told Galbraith as he looked up.

Galbraith frowned. 'And *I* think that you need someone medically qualified to make such a statement, so out of my way, please.'

Percy stood uncertainly to one side as Galbraith knelt down, did precisely what Percy had been doing when he'd arrived, then looked up and grimaced.

'You got that right, at least. Now, next question — were there any fancy almond cakes served at this recent bunfight?'

'Not that I recall,' Percy replied. 'I hadn't got that far yet, but why do you ask?'

Galbraith pointed to the discoloured drool that had dribbled down the chin of the deceased. 'There's a strong smell of almonds, which is always a dead giveaway, if you'll pardon the expression. I believe that this man was poisoned with cyanide.'

In the stunned silence that followed, the Assistant Commissioner took control. 'As the senior officer present, I'll head the necessary investigation. Before anyone can be allowed to leave, they'll need to supply statements, as I've already instructed. To save time, you can all begin by getting into pairs and taking each other's statements. Once that's completed, we'll start on the catering staff, and by then I'll have brought in some outside assistance. Let's not waste any time — set about it without delay. And it goes without saying that no-one is to eat or drink anything more in this room.'

'I wasn't joking when I said that the pork pies tasted a bit off,' Percy told Jack with a downturned mouth. 'And I should know, because I had four of them.'

'But you're still alive,' Jack pointed out, 'so it must have been in something else. But I didn't see Montague eat anything.'

'He had some beer, though,' Percy recalled. 'But so did I, and as you point out, I'm still alive. Anyway, you take my statement, then I'll take yours, and then perhaps we'll be allowed out of here.'

Percy faithfully recalled that he'd been one of the first to arrive, and had employed his charm in persuading one of the waitresses — 'a sharp-tongued, middle-aged woman called Lizzie' — to let him begin an assault on the pastries, and pull the first of the beer from the cask. 'Then I just sort of hung around, avoiding small talk with the high-rankers who sidled in here one by one, looking as guilty as schoolboys in a striptease parlour. Once you arrived, Jack, I knew I was in safe company. The rest you know for yourself, so our statements must be identical after that point.'

'I need to know how much you consumed, item by item,' Jack insisted, 'since if it *was* poison, then it was clearly in one of the foods. It can't have been in the beer, because from what I could see you had more than anyone else, and would now be *deader* than anyone else.'

'I'll tell you what I ate if you promise not to tell your aunt,' Percy said with a sigh. 'It was four pork pies, two sausage rolls, three chicken sandwiches and one of those pastries with smoked salmon stuffed into them.'

Jack couldn't help grinning; Uncle Percy had proved true to form, even on his last day. Jack then turned the police-issue notebook in which he'd been writing and pushed it towards Percy for his signature. Percy screwed up his face as he looked at what had been written on his behalf.

'Barking Grammar School has a lot to answer for — your handwriting looks like the tracks of a spider whose legs have been dipped in ink.'

'Sign the bloody thing, then you can take my statement,' Jack instructed him, and the next few minutes were occupied by Jack's recollection of having entered the proceedings when the room had been half full. He had chatted to Percy while eating a sausage roll, poured himself a beer, then taken a second sausage roll and retired to a corner of the room to await the inevitable speech.

He'd just finished signing what Percy had written down when Assistant Commissioner Bruce sidled up to them, looking slightly embarrassed.

'We couldn't find any on-duty officers of appropriate rank to take statements from the catering staff, so I'll have to prevail upon you, Chief Inspector Enright.'

'I'll lend a hand,' Percy offered, but Bruce shook his head.

'I appreciate the offer, but I have to decline, for two reasons. The first is that you retired today.'

Percy made a point of extracting his pocket watch from his waistcoat pocket and glancing down at it, before replying, 'I don't retire officially until five o'clock today — what's your second reason?'

'You're a suspect.'

'Everyone who was in this room is a potential suspect,' Percy reminded him, 'even Chief Inspector Enright here. If one suspect can take statements, surely another can do the same thing?'

'There was only one person here today about whom rude things were said by the deceased, or so I recall,' Bruce countered.

'I was only offering to be a corroborating witness, and perhaps ask the odd question of my own,' Percy persisted. 'And you admitted yourself that there aren't enough operational men left in the shop.'

Bruce thought briefly, then nodded and turned to Jack. 'Make sure that you sign off on everything the witnesses tell you, and don't let your uncle add anything of his own, got that?'

'Yes, sir,' Jack confirmed, somewhat embarrassed.

Bruce called for the waitresses to be brought back in, one by one, from the adjoining kitchen in which they'd been detained until their turn came. The first in was the lady who'd allowed Percy to access the buffet before the proceedings had even commenced, and she lost no time in reminding him of that.

'There's bloody gratitude for yer — I gives yer first knock at all the goodies, an' now yer questionin' me like I done somefin' wrong.'

'Name?' Jack asked, unmoved, and the lady transferred her aggrieved expression to him.

'Lizzie Conroy, an' I'm due on duty at the Royal Oak in twenty minutes. That's down Newgate way.'

'Address, age and occupation?'

'Forty-two, widow these five years, workin' as a barmaid to put food in the mouths of three growin' children. Angel Street,

Newgate, number sixty-eight, second floor back. Can I go now?'

'Not quite,' said Jack. 'If you're a barmaid, how come you were working here today?'

'I'm casual, like all the others bein' 'eld prisoner in the kitchen back there. We earn 'ardly anything for a day's work, an' we 'as to put up wi' cheek from the likes o' you. It ain't right, an' that's the truth.'

'So you are all casual employees hired for the event?' Jack asked by way of clarification, to a responding snort.

'Din't I just say that, cloth ears? Can I go now, or will yer give me a note for the landlord o' the Royal Oak?'

'Just one more question,' Jack said reassuringly. 'Did you see anyone put anything into any of the food and drink once it was on the table?'

'No, 'cept someone should maybe 'ave breathed a bit more life inter them 'am sandwiches what was made yesterday.'

'So you saw nobody interfering, let's say, with the food and drink supplied by your employers?' Percy added.

'Only you, yer cheeky beggar, gettin' first go at them pork pies. No wonder yer waistcoat buttons is bulgin' fit to bust.'

'Yes, thank you,' Percy replied, then he turned to Jack. 'Anything else, or can we let this good lady return to charming the patrons of the Royal Oak with her wit and wisdom?'

'No, that's all,' Jack said, before asking Lizzie to send in the next waitress.

There were five of them in all, and apart from the final one there was nothing noteworthy to report. The answers given by them all were that they were employed as casual waitresses by an organisation known as 'Strand Enterprises', which specialised in external catering and operated from a two-roomed office in Essex Street. When their services were required they'd receive a telegram from the proprietor, advising them of the date, time and location, and would be assumed to have accepted the work unless they advised their employer that they weren't available. In the main they were employed full-time as barmaids in public houses, and were taking on the extra work in order to augment their meagre incomes.

There were only two exceptions to this general description. The first was a lady who described herself as 'employed in the theatrical profession, but currently resting between engagements'. To judge by her melodramatic responses to Jack and Percy's questions, Marie Laboiselle was indeed an actress, and a very limited one in terms of ability. She couldn't offer them any new information and did nothing to alert their suspicions, so she was allowed to depart. However, the final waitress set their mental alarm bells jangling just with her name.

Mary O'Brien's Irish heritage was plainly audible as she sat before Jack and Percy, nervously twiddling the ties of her outdoor bonnet. Percy in particular set great store by the bodily demeanour of suspects and witnesses, and Mary got off to a bad start by not only playing with her headgear, but also staring intently at the floor. She gave her name in almost a whisper, and when asked to spell her surname seemed almost ashamed to own it.

'Irish?' Percy asked sharply before Jack could ask his next question.

'A long way back, to be sure,' she replied.

'How far back?' was Percy's next question as he narrowed his eyes. 'All the way back to the ferry across from Kingstown to Liverpool?'

'Dundalk,' she replied. 'Ten years an' more since.'

'Married?' Jack managed to enquire before Percy took complete control.

'Widowed,' came her reply. 'Didn't me old man suffer an accident one day when he was 'eavin' coal to keep the food on the table? He was workin' in the Poplar Dock, God preserve 'is memory, an' a bloody great load shifted sideyways, an' the poor man got buried in the stuff.'

'Poplar!' Percy snapped. 'Part of the Fenian Barracks, is it not?'

'And what would they be, exactly?' Mary asked innocently. 'Sure an' there's no soldiers around where I lives in Piggot Street.'

'Limehouse!' Percy said in triumph. 'Even better — I remember it well from my beat days, when we only went down those streets if there were four of us. As for the Fenian Barracks, it has been, for years, the centre for Irish terrorist groups who attack our troops, bomb our public buildings, then go to ground and hide themselves away inside slum tenements that are impossible for the forces of law and order to penetrate.'

'What was your late husband's name?' Jack asked, embarrassed by the ferocity of Percy's verbal attack on a frail-looking widow who was clearly apprehensive about being interviewed by two Scotland Yard officers. But then again, Percy's instincts for sniffing out lawbreakers was legendary, so perhaps he'd allow this to continue for a little while longer.

''Twas Padraig, God rest 'is soul.'

'Padraig?' Percy repeated forcefully. 'If I had a quid for every Irishman who gave the name Padraig when arrested, I could have retired years ago. It was Connor, wasn't it?'

'No, 'twas Padraig, on the grave o' me sainted mother,' Mary insisted.

Percy turned to Jack with a sneer. 'Lock her up!'

Jack looked at Percy in alarm. 'Charged with what?'

'I'll settle for the murder of Chief Superintendent Montague.'

'I never murdered nobody!' Mary protested.

'Grammatically speaking, you're correct,' Percy replied. 'You murdered "somebody", and that somebody was a former colleague of mine here at Scotland Yard. They only removed his body a few moments ago, so you missed the chance to gloat over his corpse, I'm afraid.'

'Uncle Percy, are you sure about this?' Jack asked.

Mary's eyes narrowed. 'So he's yer uncle, that it? The pair of yer puttin' the terrors on a poor widow woman what attends the Mass every day, an' twice on Sundays?'

'I'm still on the force for another ten minutes,' Percy reminded Jack, 'so if you won't put the cuffs on her, I will.' He rose to his feet with a determined frown, then walked to the doors that led into the corridor, threw them open and bellowed an instruction to the two uniformed constables who'd been brought upstairs to guard them.

'Take this woman and lock her up below stairs. Name of Mary O'Brien, and charged with the murder of Chief Superintendent Montague.'

Mary was dragged out, protesting her innocence loudly and plaintively, and calling on all the saints she knew of to observe the injustice of what was transpiring. Once the doors closed, and as her expressions of outrage became less audible as she was dragged down the hallway, Jack demanded an explanation from Percy for what seemed like an irrational antipathy towards a seemingly blameless lady.

'Montague worked in what used to be called the Irish Branch for some years,' said Percy. 'He made more enemies than you could count down in the Fenian Barracks, a rookery adjoining the Limehouse Cut, and which you no doubt learned all about when we were attached to Special Branch, chasing down gun-runners. That street in Limehouse that Mary O'Brien admits to living in is a line of slum tenements with their upper floors cleared out and levelled to allow passage between them, so that if a man goes to ground at number twenty-three, he can emerge through the back door of number thirty-seven less than a minute later, unseen by anyone in the street outside. There's a strong possibility that our Irish cousins took this opportunity to settle an old score.'

'I hope you're right,' Jack replied, 'because if not, we'll be in trouble for locking up an innocent lady.'

'She lost her innocence when she married Connor O'Brien,' Percy replied testily. 'He was the former leader of the Fenians who blew up a chamber in the House of Commons on the same night that they accounted for part of the Officers' Mess in the Tower. O'Brien went down in a hail of bullets during a street shoot-out that Montague commanded on our side a week later, and that was his widow who took her revenge this afternoon.'

'We don't know for certain that she's his widow,' said Jack, 'but it's perhaps as well that we interviewed all the others first, because you'll no doubt be insisting that we can go home now.'

'Why shouldn't we?'

'Surely we have to report our findings to Assistant Commissioner Bruce?'

'Of course we do, but not today.'

'So you're leaving me to do that on my own in the morning?'

'No,' Percy said, 'I'm delaying my retirement by another day.'

'Your dinner's in the oven,' Esther told Jack starchily as he was in the process of hanging up his overcoat in the hallway. 'It's not my fault if the mince has dried to a crust, because I expected you home on time, at least today, given that you were only showing Uncle Percy the door.'

'Wrong on both counts,' Jack said with a frown. 'First of all, he's opted to take another day in the police service, and secondly there was a murder during his farewell bunfight.'

'Are you referring to the fatal attack that Percy no doubt launched on the food supplies, or did someone actually manage to get themselves murdered during a farewell party?'

'Chief Superintendent Montague, no less,' Jack replied. 'That's why I'm late. Assistant Commissioner Bruce has taken it upon himself to head up the investigation, and Percy and I were roped in to interview the catering staff, because it looks as if poison was used. And what are those papers in your hand — more bills?'

'No, my copy of the basic teachers' manual that they gave me when I started teaching down the road. We have an inspection by Her Majesty's Inspectorate of Schools in two days' time, and I wanted to brush up on the basics.'

'But you're not a proper teacher, so why you?'

Esther sighed heavily. '*Anyone* who can control a group of more than thirty children aged from five to eight years old and persuade them to learn something is entitled to call themselves a teacher. I may officially only be classed as a "teacher's assistant", but they don't let rank amateurs loose in a classroom, not even at the Barking Board School.'

'But you only went there in the first place to control Lily and Bertie when they took their war of attrition into the classroom,' Jack reminded her. 'They're not even in your class anymore, so why are you still there?'

'Because I enjoy it, it gives me a sense of self-worth and fulfilment, and I'm not prepared to sit around here all day. And this is your second reminder of the mince that's slowly turning into a memory inside the oven, wasting gas.'

Jack removed his evening meal from the oven, gallantly ate it with a grateful smile, and left Esther to continue preparing for the school inspector's visit. Esther, for her part, read the document for the fourth time, and silently prayed for whichever patron saint looked after teachers to be at her elbow in two days' time.

It was true that she'd only joined the school as a casual, unpaid assistant when their two eldest children had become a challenge to their teacher. At the time, Esther had discovered to her delight that she had a natural gift for engaging and maintaining the interest of young children. She had therefore stayed on at the school, despite being paid a pittance in the role.

This was officially only meant to entail the laying out of books, the monitoring of children in the small playground, and calling the class register ahead of morning and afternoon sessions, but Esther did much more. Since she was not an accredited teacher, she couldn't be remunerated as such, even though her natural abilities in the classroom were regarded as a godsend to the two overworked official teachers in the rapidly growing school. Now the school was about to undergo one of the routine inspections required by law, and given that Esther had effective control of a 'primary' class, she was anxious not to let down those who had faith in her teaching abilities.

CHAPTER THREE

The following morning, Jack found Percy waiting for him in the front entrance to the Whitehall Place building that occupied half the street, known officially as 'New Scotland Yard'. He handed Jack one of the two mutton pies he'd brought in from his favourite chophouse further down along the Embankment.

'The last of a noble line, I suspect, but let's eat them in your office before we report our findings.'

Twenty minutes later they found themselves seated before the massive oak desk, behind which sat Assistant Commissioner Bruce. Jack handed over the previous day's copies from his notebook and awaited a response. When Bruce looked up, his gaze settled on Percy.

'I didn't expect to find you here, Enright,' he said.

'Many an apprehended criminal has said that over the years,' Percy replied.

'Well, your reappearance after what promises to be the shortest retirement in the Yard's history is timely, since I want you both working on this tragic outrage that resulted in the death of Montague.'

'We've already locked up the likely culprit,' Percy told him proudly.

Bruce nodded. 'So I heard, but we can't assume at this stage that it wasn't an inside job.'

'One of *us*, you mean?' Jack asked.

'That's right. All senior officers make enemies within the force — it's the inevitable outcome of having to issue unpopular orders, and discipline those who step out of line.

Very few people outside the Yard knew about yesterday's little get-together, and you two are both well placed to eliminate the horrible possibility that a valued and highly respected colleague was poisoned to death by one of our own. I want you to take apart every case that Montague worked on since rising from street constable level, and find anyone who might still hold a grudge. At the same time, I want you to scour the records for any potential grudge-bearer still on the force, or recently expelled from it. Jack, that will obviously be a task for you, given your current position at the head of manpower. As for you, Percy, you were in the service for as long, if not longer, than Montague, and I'm relying on your ability to smell out a rat.'

Early the next day, Jack was halfway through drawing up a schedule for upcoming interviews with the potential recruits for the Met when Percy arrived with a pile of files in his arms.

'I have bad news and good news,' he announced as Jack waved him into the seat in front of his desk. He dumped the files down on it, raising a cloud of dust.

'Give me the good news first,' Jack sighed, confident that if Percy said that there was also bad news, then it was almost certainly of the direst quality.

'The good news is that I managed to persuade the records clerk that I haven't yet left the force. These files on our desk are the ones that represent the most significant cases in which the late Chief Superintendent Montague was involved during his career.'

'I take it that the bad news has something to do with your reference to "our" desk?' Jack asked with a frown.

'Correct,' said Percy. 'They've already allocated mine to some jumped-up Johnny who's been newly promoted, but look on the bright side. We can work together, share ideas, and enjoy each other's company over dinner.'

'I'm not taking you as a daily guest into the Senior Officers' Dining Room, if that's what you had in mind,' Jack warned him.

Percy pulled a face. 'And I'm not prepared to relive the horrors of the "Other Ranks' Experimental Kitchen",' he insisted. 'So it looks as if Tang Li's Chophouse on the Embankment can look forward to our regular custom.'

'Esther would never let me live it down if I acquired a waistline like yours, and I think we'd both benefit from a little break from each other during the working day,' Jack suggested.

'We can negotiate that when the time comes,' Percy said breezily. 'In the meantime, how are you getting on with compiling that list of former Met officers disciplined by Montague?'

'I haven't even started,' Jack told him. 'When Bruce put me in charge of finding a possible suspect for Montague's murder, he didn't see fit to relieve me of my normal duties. This means, among other things, that you'll have to make yourself scarce when I'm conducting recruitment and potential disciplinary interviews.'

'A good job I made a start on my half of the job, then,' said Percy. 'That pile of files on our desk represents only some of those cases that may have left certain villains with a grudge against the dear departed Chief Superintendent. Care to join me in going through them?'

'If it means that *my* desk can return to normal, certainly,' Jack agreed. 'But I meant what I said about having to do my normal job on top of the additional one we seem to have acquired. So, what have we got?'

'This is my favourite,' Percy enthused as he picked up the top one. 'It records a series of armed robberies on businesses in the Docklands area roughly five years ago. Montague was Number Two in the Armed Robberies Division, and he finally got the gang surrounded when they tried to pull a daylight job on Higson's tobacco warehouse. The bond money on an incoming cargo was being stored in the office there, and someone must have got a tip-off. Anyway, to cut a long story short, one man — name of Hennessy — took the drop in Pentonville because a guard was shot dead, and three others went away for long stretches. Not as long as the stretch of Hennessy's neck, obviously, but they may all now wish they'd got the noose as well.'

'So why is it your favourite?'

'The Irish connection,' Percy said. 'It was believed at the time that the robberies were funding the Fenian mob living all around the chosen targets. And Hennessy is an Irish name, is it not?'

Jack sighed. 'Is this you trying to justify locking up that poor widow? What was her name again — O'Brien, wasn't it?'

'She was already a widow by then,' Percy told him. 'The man I believe to have been her late husband — Connor O'Brien — was shot dead the previous year. But you can't deny the Irish connection.'

'I wasn't intending to,' Jack insisted. 'It's just that before many more days are out you'll have to justify keeping the lady in custody, and so far as I can see, the only evidence you have against her is that she's Irish. Your time in Special Branch obviously left you with a prejudice against the Irish.'

'I had one long before that,' Percy said with a grimace. 'Two years of banging heads together in Fenian pubs in Bethnal

Green taught me that the Irish connection is the motivation for a good deal of the crime in the East End.'

'So is poverty,' Jack stated. 'So, what's your next favourite?'

'Our first case working as a family team,' Percy said as he peeled another file from the pile. 'Also, the case that first brought you and Esther together.'

'The Ripper?' Jack asked, marginally more interested.

'Yes. Half of Scotland Yard finished up on that one, if you remember, and Montague was no exception. He was a Detective Sergeant in those days, and if you recall there was a desperate search for anyone who might have access to knives, and a good deal of the pre-existing prejudice against Jews in Whitechapel ran to new heights. It seems that there was a formal complaint lodged against Montague for his alleged rough treatment in custody of a Jewish cobbler called Goodman. The matter was investigated, Montague was cleared of all allegations, and on his release Goodman was badly beaten by a crowd that had gathered when they'd heard of his initial arrest. He died from his injuries, and a local Jewish group vowed revenge on Montague.'

'That sounds more likely than your Fenian connection, anyway,' Jack observed drily. 'Now who the hell is *this*, further wasting my morning?'

Two men had appeared in the open doorway, hovering uncertainly. One of them was tall and gangling, with a mop of untidy red hair that drooped low on his forehead. The other was markedly shorter than his companion, with a dark fringe that looked as if it had been cut with garden shears.

'I'm Detective Sergeant Blair, sir,' said the red-haired one, 'and my companion here is Detective Constable Pinkney. Assistant Commissioner Bruce has delegated us to your team, to do what he described as the "legwork" on any enquiry you may wish to have conducted in connection with your investigation.'

'Excellent!' Percy enthused, jumping to his feet. 'Here's the first one for you to investigate. A series of bank robberies in the Docks area around Limehouse, suspected Irish connection, one man called Hennessy hanged, and two more probably still doing a long stretch in Pentonville. We need to know if there are any relatives, friends, former gang members or irate Fenians who might have been seeking revenge.'

'When he refers to "we", he means me,' Jack interjected. 'As the senior officer here, and the only one still on the permanent roll, you report to me, understood?'

'Yes, sir,' they both replied sheepishly, and the red-haired officer took the file handed to him by Percy. Once they had disappeared back down the corridor, Percy resumed the vacant seat in front of Jack's desk with a sour expression.

'That was a bit unnecessary, Jack my boy. I realise that I'm here on borrowed time, and that you consider that you've got better things to do with yours, but don't let the superior rank become a fixation. You're here today because I encouraged you to pursue a career with the police, and there are still a few things I could perhaps teach you, so don't let things go to your head.'

Jack's face reflected his contrition as he replied, 'Sorry, Uncle, but I seem to be losing control of events around me. I still have this new senior role in Recruitment and Manpower to get on top of, and matters have already begun to get behind. I've got recruitment interviews to conduct, at least one disciplinary session that I'm dreading, and now this — ferreting through long-dead files for possible lunatics with a long-standing grievance. Look, let me buy you lunch, or dinner, or whatever it's called these days, at that chophouse you mentioned.'

'It's called "luncheon" in our house,' Percy said with a frown, 'because Beattie associates with a crowd of middle-class pinched-faces from our local church who would have been comfortable in your mother's company. I still call it "dinner" out of habit. Anyway, we'll likely be dining on pork chops, or maybe baked potatoes, at a place called Tan Li's. It's a couple of hundred yards down the Embankment, if we use the rear exit from here. I'll gratefully accept your offer, once I've familiarised you with the rest of this pile — it should only take twenty minutes at most.'

'Very well.' Jack sighed as he pushed aside the papers he'd anticipated working on that morning. 'What's next?'

'Another one that might be familiar to you,' Percy told him as he extracted the next file. 'A Chinese-run pipe house — again in Limehouse — closed down by Montague at around the time that he was promoted to Chief Superintendent because he was reckoned to be unbribable. Word on the street in those days was that if you didn't take the bribe, you could expect the chop. Anyway, when Montague got this place raided and closed down, there was a warning from one of our regular street narks that the "Purple Dragon" triad had put out contracts for the deaths of all those seeking to close down their trade in opium.'

'I was lucky to escape with just a broken leg,' Jack muttered, 'and that was only because I went under a horse that bolted when the gang let off a firecracker to enable those inside the police wagon it was pulling to escape.'

'I remember you limping around the old headquarters building after that,' Percy said, 'working in Records while your leg healed. But that didn't stop you riding on the back of that coach taking a female suspect to a meeting with her lover. Remember that slum clearance fraud that her solicitor husband was up to his armpits in?'

'Some of it,' Jack replied. 'But the bright side of the broken leg was that I got to meet the Queen, who had a bravery medal pinned on my chest. She couldn't reach up high enough to do it herself, so she got her flunkey to do it instead. Then Mother treated us all to a posh meal in that fancy restaurant that Lucy knew.'

'Happy days,' Percy replied with a hint of sarcasm, 'but it's possible that Montague was still on someone's "to do" list.'

Jack shook his head. 'The Chinese gangs traditionally use hatchets to dispose of their unwanted, and any street thug seeking to claim the contract money would use a knife or a hammer. Poison is much more sophisticated.'

'You may be right,' Percy agreed reluctantly, 'but we have to explore every possibility. How about this brothelkeeper who went down for two years for purveying street urchins? Unusually, it was a male, and he threatened to get even with those officers who'd been working in plain clothes, posing as potential customers. One of them was a young Detective Constable Montague.'

'And how long ago was that?' Jack asked, unconvinced.

'Good point — it was more than twenty years ago now, so I think we can discount that one,' said Percy. 'But there are still a few more in this pile. Perhaps we'll have more luck with the internal disciplines. How long before you believe you may be in a position to start on them?'

'Tomorrow, with a bit of luck. Now, let's think of an early dinner, shall we?'

Two hours later, following a protracted meal courtesy of Tang Li, during which Percy had demonstrated precisely how a steak pie should be dealt with, Jack returned alone to his office. Percy had been persuaded to journey down to Whitechapel and enquire further into any possible remaining resentment within the Jewish community regarding the death of a local cobbler now nine years in the past. Jack was therefore free to get on with those matters that had been in abeyance all morning.

He was therefore irritated to see a fresh bundle of papers lying on his desk, with a handwritten note from Sergeant Blackwell, his personal assistant. It explained that they were the only documents that Records could come up with that related to disciplinary proceedings conducted by Chief Superintendent Montague during his thirty-three-year career.

'Could have been worse, I suppose,' Jack muttered to himself, 'but they can still wait until tomorrow.'

When Jack got home, Esther met him in the hallway with an apologetic expression on her face.

'I'm afraid it'll have to be omelette for tea. We had a teachers' meeting after school, to make sure that we had everything ready for the inspection tomorrow, and on the way home Bertie started shivering and complaining that he felt cold. I think he's gone down with the flu or something, so I'll have to leave him at home tomorrow, but Alice assures me that she can look after him as well as Miriam and Tommy. Anyway, the shepherd's pie that I was planning will have to wait until tomorrow, because I was late home with the ingredients for Polly to cook.'

'That's quite all right,' Jack assured her, grateful for the domestic help they had at the Church Lane house. 'I had a big meal with Percy in that favourite chophouse of his on the Embankment.'

'I know,' she said with a frown. 'I can smell it on your clothes. At least you picked the right evening to have a light tea.'

'I rather got the impression that *you'd* picked it,' Jack said as he walked with her into the living room, where Lily was carefully cutting pieces from some spare material left over from Esther's latest dressmaking session in order to make a smock for her favourite doll. 'Why did you need to stay for the meeting anyway?' he asked Esther. 'Isn't it just the teachers who're being inspected?'

'It's the entire school,' she replied, 'which includes me, because the current shortage of accredited teachers means that I have to take one of the infant classes. Barking's become so popular in recent years, with people taking advantage of the quick rail journey into London that you use, and the Board haven't supplied the extra teacher that we've needed for the past year or so, despite frequent requests. We're going to make that point to the inspector, in the hope that he puts pressure on them. Anyway, how was your day working alongside Uncle Percy again? Presumably there was more to it than having lunch together?'

Jack sighed. 'Far *too* much. The Assistant Commissioner's got us investigating what was almost certainly the murder by poison of the Chief Superintendent, but he hasn't relieved me of any of my normal duties. I'm slipping behind with my work, and Percy seems determined to take over leading the new investigation while I'm preoccupied with other things I should be doing.'

'Surely that's good, isn't it?'

'Not really, because the Assistant Commissioner made it very clear that I was to be in charge, and that Percy was to be kept on a short leash. That's for two reasons — first of all, he's supposed to be retired, and secondly he's a suspect.'

'Why would Percy be suspected of poisoning that Chief Superintendent?'

'You didn't hear the rude things he said about Percy — and I for one couldn't be certain that he was joking.'

'Percy seemed happy enough to be retiring, so how's he reacted to being held back from that?'

'He's as happy as a pig rolling in its own muck. It wasn't the actual investigation work that Percy had grown disillusioned with, just the politics surrounding the policing process. Percy became convinced it was all about class distinction, and holding down the masses for the benefit of the elite.'

'And what do you think?'

Jack shrugged. 'I'm not sure. Right now, I'm wondering what you were thinking of putting in the omelettes.'

CHAPTER FOUR

Esther swallowed hard as she entered the cramped all-purpose staffroom inside Barking Board School and sat down in front of the desk being occupied by Her Majesty's Inspector of Schools, James Brightside. She was the last of the staff to be interviewed, and the inspection had, so far as anyone could tell, gone better than they had feared. All the pupils had been well behaved, and the classrooms and other facilities, including the closet toilets in the shed to the rear, had been as pristine as scrubbing and last-minute rubbish removal could make them. But there still remained the difficult issue of why Esther had been teaching Primary Class One when she was only a humble teacher's assistant. Brightside opened with the obvious question, albeit with a broad smile on his face.

'You're only paid as a teacher's assistant, Mrs Enright, and yet you appear to have been carrying out teaching duties for some time. Why is that?'

'For the obvious reason, if that doesn't seem too impolite a response,' Esther replied hesitantly. 'We're at least one teacher short, despite frequent requests to the Board that governs the school. We were hoping that you could bring some pressure to bear in support of our request for an additional accredited teacher.'

'My question was more about whether or not you resent being called upon to teach when you're only being paid as an assistant,' Brightside responded.

'Far from it,' Esther replied. 'I don't need the money, because my husband is now in a senior grade in his work as a police officer at Scotland Yard, and I'm only too happy to be allowed to teach, even though I'm not accredited. Perhaps that was obvious when you watched me try to interest a group of children in the geography of Europe.'

'I was watching the pupils, not you,' Brightside told her, 'and I was happy to note the bright looks of curiosity on their faces. But I *did* note your enthusiasm — you obviously enjoy teaching.'

'I *love* it!' Esther gushed without thinking. 'I have four children of my own, two of whom are in this school, although not in my class. It comes naturally to me to be engaging young minds and helping them to learn about the world in which we live.'

'And believe me, it shows,' Brightside told her. 'In my capacity as an HM Inspector, I spend my every working day watching teachers in action. Some days I see lacklustre performances from people who obviously chose teaching because they couldn't manage anything else. That wasn't meant as an insult to teachers generally, please believe me, and certainly not to anyone I've seen at this school. My point is that in you I see a natural teacher, and one who shouldn't be hiding their light under the bushel of being merely an assistant.'

'Thank you,' Esther said, blushing. 'That means a lot, believe me. Gladys and Edmund are very kind and complimentary regarding my teaching, but of course I can't be sure that they're not just placating me because they rely on me to fill the gap with Primary One.'

'I can set your mind at rest on that score, Mrs Enright,' Brightside continued. 'I spoke confidentially to both Mrs Ayscough and Mr Browning. While they made the same point as you that the Board had left them with no option other than to put you in front of a class, they were *most* complimentary regarding your dedication and abilities as a teacher. Now, may we speak frankly?'

'I thought we were already,' Esther replied, uncertain what was coming next.

'First of all — and this must remain unofficial until my report is handed in — I intend to report *very* favourably on what I discovered here at Barking Board School, and I shall of course underline the potential difficulties that arise from being one accredited teacher short. But, perhaps inconsistently, I shall also report that the vacancy is being very ably filled by a natural teacher who lacks all but the accreditation.'

'Thank you,' Esther croaked as she felt tears of relief and gratitude welling in her eyes.

'You only have yourself to thank for what I just said,' Brightside assured her, 'but now I have to ask you why you've never taken the time to become accredited?'

'I already mentioned that I'm a mother of four,' Esther replied, 'and until now, when we've become more comfortable financially, it's never entered my head to take that step. If there comes a time when my current work is taken over by an accredited teacher, then I'll obviously experience a great sense of loss, but … well, as I just said, I hadn't got around to even thinking about it. And of course, being a housewife and mother, I couldn't begin to contemplate spending time at one of those teaching colleges.'

'That's not the only avenue into the profession,' Brightside told her, 'only the most recent one, devised by those in Parliament who've never been in front of a class in their lives. You can still qualify in the old way, which at least has the advantage of requiring actual classroom experience.'

When Esther remained silent, taking in the opportunity that might just be opening up before her, Brightside mistook her reaction for reluctance, and pressed her further.

'You could continue teaching here just as you do at present, but graded as an "assistant teacher" once you are accepted by the Accreditation Board to begin this first stage. After a given number of hours working under the supervision of an accredited teacher, and with a suitable supporting testimonial from them, you could undertake a minimum six-week course of formal training at one of the colleges. The nearest one to here is the new one in East Ham, to which you could easily travel in both directions each day. If you like the idea, would you like me to pass your name on to the Accreditation Board?'

'Oh — yes please,' Esther murmured, almost overcome by the possibilities that were running through her head. 'But I'd need to talk it over with my husband first. Not that I need his permission,' she hurried to reassure him.

'If he loves you, then he shouldn't want to stand in your way,' Brightside observed.

'That's what I always tell him,' Esther replied, 'and I've never known it to fail.'

That morning Jack had reached his office an hour early, having taken the six-twenty from Barking, rather than his usual seven-twenty, but his office was still full of police officers when he pushed open the door.

Behind his desk sat Percy, clouds of pipe smoke wafting towards the ceiling, while on the visitor side of the table sat Detective Sergeant Blair, with Detective Constable Pinkney standing beside Blair's chair. Percy slid to his feet as Jack entered, and Blair gave up his seat to him. Jack draped his overcoat over the peg provided, walked behind the desk and reclaimed his seat, which was still warm.

'Now that we appear to be observing the correct protocols,' he remarked acidly, 'to what do I owe this early start?'

'We're here with our report on that series of armed robberies that you sent us to enquire into,' Blair replied. 'The ones a few years since.'

'Five years since, as I recall,' Jack agreed, 'the final one on a tobacco warehouse that resulted in a shoot-out, a dead warehouse guard, and a hanging and several lengthy prison sentences for those involved. Chief Superintendent Montague was the one who led the charge on that occasion — am I correct?'

'In every detail, sir,' Blair replied ingratiatingly. 'And we traced those who're still doing time for that — well, at least, their wives. We can report that there appear to be no longstanding hard feelings among them regarding what happened that day. In fact, one of the wives even claimed that we'd done her a favour — that was Millie Fawcett, whose husband is doing seven years in Pentonville. Apparently he was handy with his fists, and she managed to get a divorce on the grounds of his adultery and cruelty while he was safely locked away.'

'And the other wives?' Percy prompted him.

Jack raised his eyebrows. 'They haven't already told you what they know?' he asked.

Blair shook his head before Percy could reply. 'You said that we were to report only to you, sir. Detective Inspector Enright — *this* one,' he added, with a nod towards Percy, 'was already here when we arrived not ten minutes since. He wanted to know what we'd learned, but I told him he'd have to wait. Was that in order, sir?'

'Very much in order,' Jack said with satisfaction, 'but what *about* the other wives?'

'There were two more, sir — Mary Blunt and Nell Rutherford. Mary Blunt seemingly took a ship back to where she came from originally, which was somewhere up north, maybe Newcastle. Nell Rutherford's in the women's wing of Holloway on account of her soliciting. We didn't speak to her, obviously, but she's been banged up for the past three months or more, according to the prison records.'

'What can you report, Detective Inspector?' Jack asked Percy. 'As I recall, you were going to introduce yourself to leading members of the Jewish community in Whitechapel, in order to establish whether or not the descendants of a murdered cobbler named Goodman still bore any ill will towards the man who brought about his demise.'

'And so I did,' Percy confirmed, 'and I can report that it's unlikely that whoever poisoned Montague was a relative with a grievance. Joseph Goodman's widow died last year, his son Isaac is now an optician in practice in Stepney, and his daughter Rachel married a kosher butcher from Bermondsey, and now lives south of the river. That's what I got from the neighbours anyway, and when I mentioned the unfortunate death of Goodman, only one old lady could even remember it. So I think we can rule that out as a possible line of enquiry.'

'So what do you want us to do next?' Blair asked.

'Well, it's obviously a matter for the Chief Inspector here,' said Percy with a deferential nod towards Jack, 'but my suggestion would be that we check out the claim by the lady we have in the cells, Mary O'Brien, that her husband — who she says was called Padraig — was killed in a tragic accident at Poplar Dock some years ago. Personally I don't believe a word of it, but we're no doubt going to be under pressure from up

43

top to release her before much longer. It would be nice to be able to demonstrate that she attempted to sell us a lie.'

'That sounds like a sensible way forward,' Jack agreed. 'Off you go, and report back as soon as you have something meaningful to tell us.'

Blair and Pinkney shuffled off down the hallway, and Jack and Percy decided to get a late breakfast at Tan Li's.

When they returned almost two hours later, it was to discover a note stuck to the door of Jack's office. It was a summons to Assistant Commissioner Bruce's office, timed an hour earlier. After agreeing on an alibi that they had been making joint enquiries into the backgrounds of the waitresses employed during the farewell ceremony, Jack and Percy made their way hurriedly to the top-floor suite of rooms that were made available to Bruce.

'Better late than never,' Bruce observed tersely when they were finally let into his inner office. 'I want that O'Brien woman released without delay.'

'We're in the process of checking her identity,' Jack explained, and was far from encouraged to see the senior officer's knitted brow.

'I can *tell* you her true identity,' Bruce replied coldly. 'It's Mary O'Brien, as attested by half a dozen parish priests, the Bishop of Stepney and the Chairman of the London Irish Association, all of whom have been in the ear of Commissioner Bradford, complaining of, and I quote, "the brutal and inhumane treatment of a worthy soul reduced to widowhood by a tragic accident that she humbly accepted as God's judgement on her 'wicked sin' of having missed two Masses in a row when she was bedbound with pneumonia". Relations between the force and the Irish Association are reasonably amicable at the moment, and the Commissioner is relying on me to keep things that way. So have the woman released immediately, with an apology.'

'And what if she's our poisoner?' Percy demanded.

Bruce glared at Jack. 'Does he speak for you as well, Chief Inspector, or have you taken to communicating through a ventriloquist's dummy?'

'I think he's referring to the fact that we're still completing our enquiries regarding who she claims to be,' Jack offered, then winced as Bruce brought down his fist on the desk.

'Release her by five o'clock this afternoon — or else! Dismissed!'

'Now what?' Jack asked as they made their way downstairs.

'As we were so recently reminded, you're running the show, so over to you,' Percy replied.

'Should we interview Mrs O'Brien one more time before we release her?'

'You're the one in charge, so are you asking for my advice, or what?'

'Don't come the old soldier with me,' Jack said with a sigh. 'Bruce may think of you as the monkey on the barrel organ, but I don't, so what do you think?'

'I agree with you,' Percy said.

Having been confined to a cell for three days, Mary O'Brien looked dishevelled as she was led into the room used for interviewing suspects. She sat down with a glare, and opened with, 'So you have finally come to yer senses, 'as yer? Gonna release a poor old widow woman what's missed a whole week o' Masses, an' whose immortal soul is no doubt in urgent danger o' fallin' inter the pit?'

'The Bishop of Stepney seems to believe in your innocence, anyway, so you can light a candle in his sacristy when you call in to thank him,' Percy muttered. 'I'm not so easily taken in, so tell us again why you were serving at the farewell party where a senior officer was poisoned.'

'Like I told you both already,' Mary insisted, 'I'm just a poor widow earnin' an honest livin' servin' the Devil's brew to wicked souls in order to keep the wolf from the door.'

'Do you not have any other means of employment?' Jack asked.

'I does some cleanin' work around the parish, an' the bishop relies on me for washin' 'is 'oly vestments from time to time. But I'm not like all them other hussies what sells their souls workin' in dens o' iniquity where men goes to drink away their wages.'

'So how did you get to be working as a casual waitress?' Percy asked.

'I were told about this office in Essex Street what needed cleanin', by a woman what goes to the same church as me — Christ Church, in Greyfriars — an' what used to do it 'til 'er knees got too bad. So I got to do it, an' the man what runs the business there asked me if I'd like to earn an extra quid a day servin' sandwiches and the like at private parties. The tricky gombeen never mentioned that I'd also be servin' the Devil's brew, but I penances myself for that after every time, an' the money can sometimes make all the difference.'

'Tell us more about this "gombeen", as you call him,' Jack invited her.

Mary shrugged. 'Nice enough feller what was once better positioned in life, but now 'as to rely on sendin' the likes o' me out to parties an' suchlike. Mr Spencer, we calls 'im, an' so far as I know the business 'e runs is honest.'

'And the name of his business?' Percy asked.

I think it's "Strand Enterprises", or somethin' like that,' Mary replied. 'That's the name on the door, anyways. Yer might want to get 'im to confirm what I'm tellin' yer, then maybe I can go back 'ome, where me cat must be 'alf dead with starvation by now.'

'You're free to go now,' Jack told her, 'and we apologise for any misunderstanding regarding your identity.'

'Apology accepted,' Mary replied, then nodded at Percy. 'Although yer Dad don't look ser pleased to be seein' the back o' me.'

'He's my uncle, not my father,' Jack corrected her with a smile.

'Well, I'll still light a candle for yer,' said Mary, ''cos bein' related familywise with 'im in *any* way can't be good for the soul.'

CHAPTER FIVE

It was Sunday lunchtime in the old family home in Church Lane, and Jack and Esther were hosting one of the family get-togethers that were all too rare these days. Sunday lunch at Church Lane had been unofficially compulsory up until the previous year, when the matriarch of the family, Constance Enright, had died, and somehow the tradition had fallen into abeyance. The estate had been amicably divided between Jack and his sister Lucy, with Jack conveying, free of charge, he and Esther's former house around the corner in Bunting Lane to Lucy, her husband Teddy and their three children. They used it as a weekend retreat from the noise and bustle of London, where Teddy maintained a successful architectural practice in Holborn.

In exchange, Lucy had assigned her share of the old family home to Jack, and the four children born to him and Esther were now consorting happily with their three cousins in the garden. They were dressed in their play clothes and indulging in their favourite 'castles and dungeons' game that had been made possible by the construction of a climbing frame and platform in the centre of the lawn.

Lucy and Teddy and their family had been staying overnight in their weekend home round the corner. The only ones who'd been obliged to travel out of London for the excellent rack of lamb that Polly had cooked, were Percy and his wife Beatrice.

'Teddy would never try to prevent me following my theatrical dreams,' Lucy cooed as she reached out for the hand of her husband, who was sitting next to her at the table.

'I wouldn't dare,' Teddy murmured in reply, to polite chuckles all round.

'In my younger days, there was no question of a wife going out to work, at least not in our social class,' Beattie said. 'Being a wife, and then usually a mother, was regarded as a full-time occupation in itself. The only women in polite society who were actually required to earn a living were those who remained unmarried. They often took to being governesses or schoolteachers, just as Esther's contemplating, although of course she's doing so from choice and not necessity.'

Esther had proudly announced, during the pre-lunch sherries, that following the inspection of Barking Board School she'd received a letter inviting her for an interview in two days' time with the regional Teachers' Accreditation Board. It would take place at the newly opened East Ham Teacher Training College, which she might one day be attending as a student teacher, once she'd served enough qualifying hours of practical teaching in Barking. The reaction had been overwhelmingly supportive, particularly from her sister-in-law Lucy, who spent her leisure hours as an enthusiastic and broadly admired member of the Holborn Players Amateur Theatrical Group.

'That's all very well for ladies who enjoy a certain degree of financial security,' Percy put in, 'but for those who do not — working-class widows and the like — life is far from being so easy. Jack and I spent part of the week interviewing women of that sort who, in addition to having to work behind the bars of public houses, were reduced to earning an extra pound — literally, only a pound — on their feet serving sandwiches, pastries and beer at private functions such as my retirement do. Their boss is a private contractor who no doubt enjoys a fat profit at their expense.'

'Here endeth the lesson,' Beattie muttered, then turned to Percy. 'Save all that Socialist claptrap for work, dear. You're with family now, and we don't need to hear it. You'll have plenty of future opportunities, given your stubborn refusal to retire when it was handed to you on a plate.'

It was a bone of contention in the Enright house in Hackney that Percy had, to Beattie's mind anyway, deliberately avoided having to spend more retirement time with her, when there were so many tasks that needed his attention around the house. She'd also been hoping to involve him more in her various church groups.

'It was hardly Uncle Percy's fault that someone was murdered at his farewell party,' Jack pointed out, 'and it's quite a feather in *both* our caps that the Assistant Commissioner selected us to head up the investigation into it.'

'According to Percy, you've made little headway yet,' Beattie replied sourly, 'or is that just Percy seeking to justify his continued absence from home?'

'No, he's correct, I'm afraid,' Jack admitted. 'It's been just under a week now — a week on Wednesday, as it happens — and all we've done is eliminate a few waitresses and re-investigate some of the cases that the deceased had worked on.'

'I know that Constance had a strict rule that there was to be no shop talk around the meal table,' Teddy recalled, 'but presumably that rule no longer applies. What you've briefly alluded to sounds fascinating, and I for one would love to learn more about it. There was a murder at Percy's farewell send-off, is that right?'

'Only too right,' Percy confirmed. 'The victim was the man who was giving *me* the kiss of death, as it transpired.'

'What he means,' Jack said, 'is that the murder victim was Chief Superintendent Montague who was the ultimate boss for both of us, and to whom therefore fell the task of saying nice things about Uncle Percy. It was a very short speech.'

'And a very rude one,' Percy snorted, 'so rude, in fact, that I became an immediate suspect when someone dosed his beer with cyanide.'

'We don't know that it was his beer,' Jack reminded him.

Percy frowned. 'You were the one who pointed out that you didn't see Montague eat anything, so the poison must have been in his beer.'

'And since you presumably sampled at least two of everything edible,' Beattie chimed in knowingly, 'we can reliably conclude that it wasn't in the food.'

'I also had a few beers myself,' Percy admitted, 'so if it *was* in the beer, then someone must have slipped it into Montague's glass. I probably had a narrow escape myself, come to think of it — my glass was left on the buffet table when we stepped forward for the speech at the lectern, so they could have poisoned mine as well.'

'Where did Montague leave *his* glass?' Esther asked.

Jack's eyes opened wide as he followed her line of thought. 'He left it alongside yours, didn't he?' he asked Percy. 'I have a memory of the two of you putting your glasses down and walking to that lectern for the farewell speech. Esther has raised a new possibility — over to you, Esther, if you're thinking what I'm thinking.'

'*You* may have been the target,' she said to Percy.

He looked stunned. 'Who'd want to do away with me?'

'Your silence at this moment would be greatly appreciated, all of you,' Beattie said laconically.

'It's a good point, though,' Jack persevered. 'We've been assuming all along that Montague was the victim, but supposing that whoever was responsible mistook his glass for yours? They were next to each other on the trestle table, weren't they?'

'Tricky things, poisons,' Lucy suddenly added. 'In *Hamlet* — by Shakespeare, of course — there's a scene at the end where Laertes, whose girlfriend Ophelia and father Polonius have both been killed by Hamlet, decides to kill Hamlet by poisoning the tip of his sword and challenging Hamlet to a duel. Somehow or other the swords get switched, and both men die from the poison that was only intended for one. It's always a difficult scene to stage.'

There was a respectful silence around the table while everyone considered that possibility.

'Starting tomorrow, we'd better start looking closely at anyone who might have been harbouring a long-standing grudge against you,' Jack said to Percy.

'You'll need more than a week,' Beattie said with a sigh, 'and if he's not finally retired by the end of the month, you can add me to the list of suspects.'

On Monday morning, back in his office, Jack finally steeled himself for the task he'd been putting off for at least a week. Constable Jennings was summoned for the interview that would almost certainly end his brief career, and it would fall to Jack to deliver the blow.

Although Percy had retired as the inspector in charge of the Discipline Branch, he had been instantly replaced by a newly promoted Inspector Walter Medley. His task was to investigate alleged wrongdoings by professional colleagues, then make a provisional decision regarding the appropriate punishment if the man was indeed guilty. If his initial conclusion was that the offender should be dismissed from the force, then that decision had to be endorsed by Jack, as head of Recruitment and Manpower. Albert Jennings had been summoned to an interview with Jack, with Medley in attendance, in order to learn his fate.

At the appointed hour Medley and Jennings knocked on his door, and Medley took the spare seat in front of Jack's desk while Constable Jennings stood, ramrod straight, in front of it. Jack was as familiar with the facts of the case as six readings of Medley's report could make him, and he frowned as he made a pretence of reading it yet again.

Jennings had been, for the past six months, a beat constable attached to H Division in Whitechapel, Jack's old stomping ground during his uniform days. That particular area of the East End was close to the London Docks, with an itinerant and multinational workforce that caused considerable difficulties for the authorities when they went in search of relaxation. The division was known to contain well over a thousand 'unfortunates', including prostitutes either maintaining a precarious living or financing an alcohol or drug addiction. When possible, if only for administrative convenience, the police on beat patrol turned a blind eye to furtive goings-on up side alleys.

But not always. Sometimes it was necessary to 'run in' a street prostitute if she was causing public offence, for example by loudly proclaiming her services in a crowded thoroughfare during daylight hours, or creating a disturbance when arguing with a 'mark' regarding the non-delivery of her 'present'. The result was that it was left in the discretionary hands of beat constables whether or not to take the women into custody and charge them with a crime. For many of the women, this resulted in either a fine they could not afford, or a short prison sentence that would briefly eliminate their ability to earn their livelihood.

The women knew all about this discretionary power. It was rumoured that they regularly played upon it by offering a constable, in lieu of a 'running-in', the sort of service, this time free of charge, that they'd been caught delivering. It also exposed the women to the possibility of a financial bribe, and most of them knew which officer was open to a bribe of either type.

Constable Jennings had been almost unbelievably stupid in not only seeking, and receiving, financial bribes, but then also taking the women into custody charged with soliciting, in order to make himself look efficient in the exercise of his duties. A group of prostitutes, led by one of the most vociferous of their number called Maisie Hoxton, had lodged a formal complaint against Jennings that consisted of an allegation that he'd been soliciting bribes. The complaint had been sponsored by local clergymen working in an outreach centre established in the hope of taking unfortunates off the streets. This couldn't be ignored by the Divisional Inspector, who'd had Jennings covertly followed by an officer from another division disguised as a street sweeper. Inspector Medley had no reason to doubt the truth of the complaint, particularly when Jennings had offered no evidence — even a character reference — to refute it.

Jack looked up helplessly from the report and asked the most obvious question that came to mind. 'Why?'

'Beg pardon, sir?' Jennings asked.

'What possessed you to do something so stupid, not to mention unlawful?'

'The money, sir,' Jennings replied.

'*Obviously* it was for the money,' Jack replied sharply, 'but why were you so desperate as to take such an obvious risk?'

'For our Jimmy, sir — he's only two, and our only child. He's got something called "consumption", and we've been told that he'll die if we don't get him a bed in a sanatorium. But they cost more money than I earn, and the missus just lost her job in the factory, on account of the time she's had to take off to look after Jimmy, sir. So I can only hope that you can see your way clear to giving me a formal reprimand to go on my record, rather than sacking me. We need the money, you see?'

Jack swallowed the urge to take the soft option. This sort of dishonesty by police officers on the front line, if allowed to escalate, could grow to epidemic proportions. It was his duty to constitute the thin line of defence.

'Dismissed from the force, with effect from today,' he announced coldly as he closed the report file and handed it to Inspector Medley, who smiled with a smug satisfaction that Jack was severely tempted to wipe away with his fist.

As the door closed behind them, Jack let out a long sigh of relief and finally made a start on the disciplinary files that had involved the late Chief Superintendent Montague, and which had been lying on his desk for three days.

There weren't many of them, but each might have given rise to resentment on someone's part. First on the pile was a case going back three years, to 1895, when Montague had been second in command in the Armed Robbery Division of Scotland Yard. He had accused an armed Detective Constable called Claude Simpson of cowardice when he'd disobeyed an order to enter the back room of a department store in Regent Street, in which armed gunmen had taken refuge after the alarm had gone off, along with two shopgirls they'd taken hostage.

The two young women had fortunately been released before the robbers had escaped over a rear wall, and Simpson had explained that he had not attempted to rescue them beforehand because his weapon had jammed while he'd been trying to fire off a warning shot prior to entering the back room. Montague had refused to accept this as an excuse, even after a firearms expert had confirmed that the revolver in question — a standard Webley issued to all qualified officers when appropriate — was prone to jamming. Simpson had been demoted back down to uniform duties in a local division, and had resigned from the force six months later. Jack made a note to get Blair and Pinkney to enquire as to what he had done for a living thereafter, since that sort of resentment could easily fester until it became murderous in nature.

There was little likelihood that the man involved in the next case had taken his revenge in person, since he would have needed to do so from beyond the grave. However, Detective Sergeant Herbert Gilbert might well have left aggrieved relatives behind after his suicide when demoted to Detective Constable for alleged insubordination towards Chief Superintendent Montague. Gilbert had disobeyed orders to close down a covert surveillance operation at the Albert Dock that had been on the point of netting those behind a conspiracy to import opium. By the time the gang responsible had been caught in a new surveillance operation ordered by another senior officer two months later, it had been estimated that over a hundred additional lives had been lost to the vile substance, and Gilbert had hung himself. 'More work for Blair and Pinkney,' Jack muttered as he reached for the next file.

This one definitely looked more promising, at least on a cursory read-through. Constable Thomas Benton, B Division, Westminster, had been thrown out of the force following an investigation headed by Montague. It had been alleged that Benton had sexually molested young women from the various organisations that had staged protest meetings outside the Houses of Parliament in support of their demand for equal voting rights with men. The allegations against him, involving eight women in total — three of whom had lodged their complaints through solicitors — were that while conducting them down into the cells of the local police station, Benton had taken the opportunity to sexually assault them. On one occasion, fellow officers had had to intervene when a lady in her late twenties had been about to be raped. This had led to an internal enquiry, to which were added the various complaints already on file.

Jack's curiosity was drawn to a final, handwritten entry dated several months after Benton's dismissal. It had been written at the foot of the disciplinary record, and read simply: *Died, Brick Lane, August 1894.*

He was just trying to recall why the name of that street was so familiar when the door opened and Percy strode in with another armful of files, then took the visitor's chair that had recently been occupied by Inspector Medley.

'Time to eliminate me as a suspect, while at the same time considering me as a potential victim,' he announced gleefully. 'That's before we have dinner; hopefully this task will reduce your appetite, because it's my turn to pay.'

'Where do you want to start?' Jack asked. 'And have we got the week free to wallow in the mire of your service career?'

'We might look first at those cases that might have left me with enemies *outside* the force, before we take on the far more difficult task of considering the ones I made while conducting disciplinary hearings.'

'I've just had to sign off on one,' Jack grimaced. 'How did you manage to preserve your sanity?'

'Some would argue that I didn't,' Percy said, 'but let's not get distracted. Who might still bear me a grudge for just doing my job?'

'It rather depends on *how* you did it,' Jack replied. 'I can clearly recall two offenders — by which I mean those who offended *you* — whose families might harbour a lingering resentment over the fact that they never made it to trial alive.'

'If you're referring to that repulsive and overbearing art dealer who went under a goods train when he was trying to escape from the trap I'd set him —' Percy began, only to be silenced by a raised hand.

'As I recall,' Jack said, 'the only relative who might have mourned his passing was no longer alive when he died, for the logically impeccable reason that she'd been his victim, as well as being his sister. Not even his young employee had a good word to say about him, so I think we can rule out any revenge arising from that case.'

'What, then?' Percy challenged him.

'How about that dreadful man you first of all collared, then exposed to the Bethnal Green mob that he'd been terrorising for some time? Some sort of rehousing programme by London City Council, wasn't it? It was around the time that I was confined to Records with a broken leg, but you persuaded me to jump onto the back of a cab in Hampstead, while you talked Esther into posing as a seamstress in the house of some snooty solicitor. Can you recall that case, or does your conscience have a "limitations" period?'

Percy chuckled. 'You're thinking about Michael Maguire, or "Mangler" as he was affectionately known. He was the enforcer for a grubby outfit that had bought up whole portions of Bethnal Green once it became known that London County Council were planning to redevelop it. The properties were tenanted at the time, but Maguire — working under the name "Michael Truegood" — was hired to frighten entire families out of their homes, so as to give his employers vacant possession when the time came to sell the land to the LCC at a massive profit. Those who refused to leave were done to death messily with heavy equipment that also came in handy for the demolition jobs.'

'It's slowly coming back to me,' Jack said. 'But didn't Maguire come to a sticky end before he even got to trial?'

'Yes, most unfortunate,' said Percy. 'He was being transferred from the local pork shop to Newgate when the mob, who somehow knew of the planned transfer, ambushed the transfer party and stoned him to death in the street. There were those who made the unworthy suggestion that I'd somehow been responsible for that.'

'And is it possible that someone is seeking revenge for his death?'

Percy gave a dismissive snort. 'There can't have been a living soul in Bethnal Green at that time who mourned Maguire's death. As you just accurately recalled, it was the people of Bethnal Green who brought it about, so why blame me? At the worst, I simply provided them with the opportunity, and after all those deaths he caused in Short Street and Brick Lane, who can blame them?'

Jack's mouth dropped open. 'Did you say Brick Lane?'

'Yes — that was one of those streets in which a spate of horrible deaths occurred, all engineered by Maguire. Why?'

Jack slid the disciplinary report relating to Thomas Benton across the table. 'Read the final entry in that report, then tell me if *you* have any appetite left.'

CHAPTER SIX

'I still reckon it's just pure coincidence,' Percy announced dismissively as he carved into his first pork chop with the enthusiasm of a tree-feller and the accuracy of a surgeon.

'And I maintain that we can't just ignore it,' Jack insisted. 'It's the first thing we've come up with that links back to a previous case, and therefore a motive for murder.'

'But whose murder?' Percy challenged him. 'So Benton died in Brick Lane at the same time that Maguire was disposing of tenants who refused to move out — so what? If he left a widow, or some other aggrieved relative, then surely the person to take revenge on would be Maguire, and the street mob did that for them.'

'We don't know why Benton was in Brick Lane in the first place,' Jack cautioned. 'Perhaps, after being thrown out of the police force, he was hired by Maguire to do dirty deeds. Or perhaps he was hired by nervous tenants to protect them from Maguire's bullies. We just don't know what connection he had with Brick Lane.'

'Perhaps he lived there himself, and became just another victim of the reign of terror and intimidation,' Percy suggested, 'in which case, we're back to the argument that Maguire was the obvious one to take revenge on.'

'It's not that simple,' Jack persisted. 'Benton was a constable in B Division, working the Westminster and Pimlico beats. Why would he be living in Bethnal Green?'

'I haven't the faintest idea. Do you think we should have pudding after this?'

'You can if you like, but don't try to evade the issue at hand. What's the connection between Benton and Brick Lane?'

'You're assuming that there is one, or rather that there once *was* one. The entire case goes back three years, remember? And isn't that why Bruce allocated those two gawky detectives to our team? Blair and Pinkney? Perhaps we should get them to make enquiries into something that's almost ancient history, if you're that convinced that we should be following it up.'

'I've already got enough for them to do, arising from the reports I read earlier today of disciplinary proceedings that Montague was involved in.'

'Then perhaps you should go down there yourself and start asking awkward questions.'

'I don't really know the area, and it was once your patch, as I recall from what Montague told us during your premature retirement.'

'All the more reason for me to stay well away from there,' Percy retorted as he pushed the empty plate to one side. 'Apart from my undoubted lingering unpopularity as a beat bobbie all those years ago, there may still be someone down there with a grudge against me for queering the pitch on what was, until I stuck my nose in, a *very* profitable fraud.'

'If nothing else,' Jack reasoned, 'it can't do any harm to dig out your old case file.'

'Do what you like — right now I'm going to have plum pudding with custard.'

They found Blair and Pinkney hovering in the hallway outside Jack's office when they returned from lunch.

'I was wondering when we'd see you two again,' Jack muttered as he turned the key in the lock. 'Come inside and tell us what you discovered regarding the death of Padraig

O'Brien, which so far as I recall was the only job I allocated to you.'

'It took a while to persuade the Poplar Dock management to allow us to go through their records,' Blair explained. 'They're very sensitive about deaths on their premises, and I think they were worried that we were treating the death as a murder. But we got there in the end.'

'And?' Jack asked impatiently.

'And Padraig O'Brien did indeed die as the result of a shifting coal cargo that he was heaving as part of a squad hired for the day. Two years ago, it was — I've got the date here, if you want it.'

'It still doesn't prove that he was married to that Mary O'Brien who Bruce released against my better judgement,' Percy growled. 'She could have heard about his death — and bear in mind that the Irish community's a very tight one — and simply chosen to assume the identity of his tragic widow.'

'There *was* a widow, who received what in the circumstances must be considered a very paltry payout following Padraig's death,' Blair added, then looked down at his notes. 'Her name *was* Mary, right enough.'

'They're *all* bloody well called Mary in the Irish community!' Percy objected.

Blair frowned. 'Not my mother — her name was Bridget, although Dad called her "Bridie".'

'You're Irish?' Percy asked, surprised. 'How did you finish up with a name like Blair, if you're Irish?'

'They allow mixed marriages over here,' Blair replied. 'My father's Scottish.'

'And do you live down in the Docks area?' Percy demanded. 'If so, that's something we might be able to take advantage of in this case.'

Blair sighed. 'You're letting your prejudice get the better of you. I was brought up in Stepney, and now I live in Clerkenwell.'

'So did I, once,' Jack told him with a smile, and Percy left it at that.

'So what's next?' Blair asked.

Jack pushed a bundle of files towards him. 'Some follow-up work on various disciplinary files that Chief Superintendent Montague was involved with at one time or another. First is the matter of the suicide of Herbert Gilbert, after he was disciplined for disobeying Montague and closing down of a drugs surveillance operation in Albert Dock. We needn't go into *why* he ended his life — I just need to know if there's a vengeful widow hiding in the shrubbery. Then there's the more recent employment history of Claude Simpson, formerly of the Armed Robbery Squad, who was demoted back down to uniform, again for reasons we needn't go into, except that he was perhaps unfairly branded as a coward, after which he resigned. He may still be burning with resentment, and I want to know where he is now and what he's doing for a living.'

'Very well, we'll get straight onto both matters,' Blair announced as he took the files and turned to leave.

'Hang on,' Jack instructed him. 'I haven't finished. This third one looks particularly promising — to my mind anyway, although Inspector Enright has a different opinion. Three years ago, he investigated — very successfully — a racket in Bethnal Green at a time when they were clearing out the old slums in order to build new houses. A gang was sent in to put the frighteners on those tenants who refused to move out, thus leaving the company that owned the land with the unencumbered freehold when they sold the land to the council for a huge profit. That's just the general background, so don't worry about trying to absorb it all. What I want from you is all the detail you can get on a man called Thomas Benton, a former B Division constable who was found dead in Brick Lane during that time. He wasn't one of the tenants who refused to move, so I need to know why he was in Brick Lane, and why he died. Ask around, but you should know that the thug who was behind the tenant murders was a man called Michael Maguire, and he came to a sticky end when a street mob got hold of him. My instinct tells me that Benton's death wasn't necessarily a tenant murder, and that Maguire may have had nothing to do with it, so I want you to dig below the surface and come up with the *real* reason for Benton's death.'

As Blair and Pinkney departed, Percy said, 'At least that'll keep them out of our hair for a day or so, but I still say it's a wild goose chase. Anyway, what's next in the two hours remaining of the afternoon?'

'I'm going to send for the full file on that Bethnal Green fraud, in case I've missed something significant,' Jack replied. 'Then I'm going to take it home to read, and get on the good side of Esther, who's got an important day ahead of her tomorrow. It's not every day I can go home early, while still doing my job. I suggest that you walk off all that food you ate.'

The following morning, a few minutes before eleven, Esther alighted from the horse bus that had taken less than fifteen minutes to cover the two miles or so from the centre of Barking to the stop on East Ham High Street that she'd been told to ask for. It was located immediately in front of the newly constructed three-storey brick building that housed, among other things, the teacher training college that she might one day be attending in order to convert her practical classroom experience into a formal teacher accreditation.

She walked through the doors into a broad hallway that was full of the sound of students of various ages hurrying between classes, and made a mental note that off to her left there appeared to be a cafeteria where she could no doubt acquire a cup of tea after her interview. As instructed in the letter she had received, she presented herself at the enquiries desk off to her right and proudly announced that she was here for an interview with the North London Teachers' Accreditation Board.

'Name?' the lady behind the desk asked as she consulted what looked like quite a long list.

'Esther Enright,' Esther replied, eyeing the list a little apprehensively. Those interviewing her could no doubt afford to be choosy.

'Down the main hallway, take the stairs at the end up one flight, then take the right-hand corridor down to Room 217, and take a seat outside,' she was told as her name was ticked off the list.

Outside Room 217 was a row of chairs, four of which were already occupied by nervous-looking individuals who Esther assumed were fellow applicants for teacher registration, one of them an earnest-looking young man. One by one they were called in by a young woman armed with a list. After what seemed like only ten minutes per interview, each of them was ushered back out into the corridor by the same young woman.

After a short while, the young woman opened the door, popped her head round it and called for Esther. Taking a deep breath and assuming a broad smile, Esther walked behind the usher into a small room that contained only a desk with three people seated behind it, and a chair in front of it that she was invited to occupy.

While the two men on either side of the early middle-aged lady in the centre shuffled their papers, the woman introduced herself. 'I'm Emily Allsop, Principal of the East Ham Teacher Training College. The gentleman on my right is Mr Edward Mulberry, District Administrator of the School Boards' Administration Branch of the Education Department, and on my left is Mr Herbert Duckworth of the London School Board. I'll invite them to open this interview with a few preliminary questions.'

The man on the right, as viewed by Esther, cleared his throat noisily, narrowed his eyes and asked, 'Does your husband approve of your ambition to become a teacher?'

'Of course,' Esther replied, doing her best not to grit her teeth. 'We agree on everything in our joint life.'

'So he would not object to you abandoning your children in order to become a full-time teacher?'

'They would not be abandoned,' Esther countered with just a hint of disapproval, 'any more than they are at present, when I undertake my current teaching duties in the local school. My two oldest are of school age anyway, while the younger two are adequately supervised by a live-in domestic servant.'

'You are already teaching, I note,' the second man observed as he took over from the first. 'Why are you seeking accreditation?'

'I'm only a teacher's assistant at present, and I'm only employed to teach because the size of the intake at Barking Board School exceeds the capacity of the two existing teachers, despite regular requests for an additional teacher to be supplied. When and if that occurs, I will be back to being a teacher's assistant.'

'And you'll no doubt miss the income from being a full-time teacher?' the same man asked.

Esther shook her head. 'When I said that I was "employed" as a teacher, I was referring to what I do in practice. I'm only *paid* as a teacher's assistant.'

'So you are seeking additional income from teaching?'

'To be honest, the income aspect is almost an irrelevance,' Esther replied. 'My husband's salary is such that we do not require a second one.'

'And what is your husband's occupation?'

'He's the first ever Chief Inspector to have been appointed inside Scotland Yard, and he's in charge of all recruitment for the Metropolitan Police.'

In the taut silence that followed, Emily Allsop inclined her head for silent confirmation that neither of the men had any further questions, then asked Esther gently, 'What makes you feel that you'd make a good teacher?'

Esther thought for a moment, then opted for honesty. 'If it doesn't sound too immodest, I feel that I'm already quite good at it, and I'm seeking to become accredited in order to learn what might be missing from my teaching skills. At present, I can only go on my instincts.'

'And what guides those instincts?'

'The reaction of the children I teach. I always seem to be able to maintain their interest, and I'm fortunate not to endure any bad behaviour in class, which in my experience is engendered by boredom.'

'Could you perhaps give us an example of how you manage to retain the interest of a class of, say, eight-year-olds?' Emily Allsop requested.

Esther thought back to something she'd been doing the previous week. 'I should perhaps mention that the constraints placed upon us by the high number of students in my primary class mean that I have to teach a mixed group aged from five to eight years in age. But all children enjoy games — particularly competitive ones. I learned that from my own children, so I make a game of everything I teach. For example, last week I was teaching them the geography of England, and I made a large map that showed all the major towns in the nation without naming them. Then I began with the pupil who's proved to be the brightest in my group, and told him that he was the first on an imaginary "magic bicycle", and would remain on it for as long as he could name the next town on the line that I'd drawn between the towns. He guessed Luton, because his grandmother lives there, but he couldn't go any further, so we wrote "Luton" above the town. Then little Sarah could identify Northampton, where she sometimes goes for a holiday with her cousins, and she was then on the magic bicycle. I won't bore you with the rest of it, but it proved very effective in encouraging the children to absorb information.'

'If you were to be offered a place on one of our six-week courses,' Emily began, 'when would you be free to start? The next one commences on the first Monday of next month, which is *next* Monday.'

'So soon?' Esther asked, genuinely concerned. 'I wouldn't want to leave my colleagues in Barking in the lurch. And I'll need to acquire the necessary teaching hours before I'll be qualified for admission.'

'You already have sufficient,' Emily told her, 'and we could supply a replacement for you in Barking from the large number of students enrolled on our full-time course who have yet to acquire any practical experience. So on that understanding, could you start next Monday?'

'Yes, of course,' Esther replied, rendered almost breathless by the direction that the conversation had suddenly taken.

Emily Allsop said something under her breath to the other two that sounded like an enquiry, and they both nodded. Then she turned back to grace Esther with a broad smile and requested that she return to her seat outside.

Back in the corridor, Esther was wondering what she might have said to ruin her chances. None of the others had been held back after their interview, and hers had seemed even briefer than theirs. She was therefore quite anxious when the door opened to reveal Emily Allsop, who told the three other potential candidates awaiting interview that the panel was taking a thirty-minute break. Emily then smiled at Esther and asked, 'Would you care for a cup of tea?'

Ten minutes later, Esther returned from a much-needed visit to the private bathroom attached to Emily Allsop's office, and was immediately served with a cup of hot, sweet tea.

'I congratulate you on the way you dealt with those old fossils on either side of me,' said Emily warmly. 'They're only in positions of authority in the education world because they couldn't make it in the War Office and the Treasury respectively. They believe that a woman's place is in the home, but you clearly demonstrated the opposite. I've never known Herbert Duckworth to give up after only two questions.'

'I've learned the hard way,' Esther said. 'As a Jewish girl living in the East End, and taking in sewing for a living, I soon had to learn to stand up for myself.'

'Believe me, it shows,' Emily replied. 'And presumably you'll put your husband in his place if he tries to prevent you from coming here every day for a month?'

'He'll know better than to even think of doing that,' Esther giggled, 'but does that mean I've been given a place on the course? And isn't it actually six weeks long?'

'Of *course* you've been accepted, and I'm sorry if I didn't say so formally. As for the length of your studies, it falls to me to determine when a student qualifies for accreditation, and in your case I'm almost embarrassed to ask you to even consider a month. I've never interviewed a more natural and worthy candidate, and what a refreshing change you were from some of the others, who are only interested in a respectable career with a *very* modest income, and in the main wouldn't last five minutes in the real world.'

'So I start next Monday?'

'Indeed you do. You'll be receiving a letter from me, formally inviting you onto the course, and advising you of what you'll need to bring with you. Now, I must get back to some more no doubt dreary interviews.'

Esther almost felt like bursting into song as she stepped back out into the warm midday sunlight and crossed the road to await the horse bus that would take her home to Barking.

CHAPTER SEVEN

Sitting in his office, Jack finally got around to opening the file that he'd taken home with him the previous evening. He had been unable to read it because Esther had insisted that he test her on all the questions she might be asked during her interview for teacher training the following day. He'd been only too happy to show her some support, because being a teacher obviously meant a lot to her. He wondered how she might be feeling right now as he took out his fob watch and noted that it was approaching nine o'clock. Esther would by now be kissing Miriam and Tommy goodbye, and hopefully Lily and Bertie had accepted that today they would be accompanied by Alice for the daily walk to their school.

With a wistful sigh he opened the file and relived the days three years ago, when Percy had begun investigating a series of unexplained and violent deaths in the general area of the Old Nichol in Bethnal Green, while accepting the additional, and unofficial, task of searching for a missing girl called Emily. She had been working as a nanny to two infants in the Hampstead house of a wealthy solicitor called Spencer Mallory, and she had disappeared at the same time as the two children in her care. She was the niece of Jack and Esther's upstairs neighbour at the time, and they had persuaded a reluctant Percy to investigate her disappearance.

But, by a strange quirk of fate, Percy had learned that Emily's employer, solicitor Spencer Mallory, was one of those behind a company called Gregory Properties, which had been buying up slum houses in Bethnal Green that were due for demolition ahead of a revolutionary public housing project planned by

London County Council. His partner in that firm, Victor Bradley, had been employed by the Planning Department of the LCC. Therefore, Bradley had been well placed to ensure not only that Gregory Properties were aware in advance of the proposals for Bethnal Green, but also that they would be guaranteed a fat profit when the land was sold on to the council with vacant possession.

Although Percy had originally only been tasked with investigating the brutal murders of the few remaining tenants who couldn't be frightened into moving out ahead of the sale of the land to the council, he had clearly identified a massive fraud, and a blatant piece of civic corruption. This had led to prison sentences for both Mallory and Bradley — seven years for Bradley, but only two for Mallory in exchange for his testimony against Bradley, and to reflect the loss of his professional status as a consequence of his conviction.

Jack chuckled as he recalled that the motivation for Mallory to 'peach' on Bradley had not simply been a desire to reduce his own sentence, for it had emerged that Bradley had been conducting an illicit affair with Mallory's wife for some years, and was in fact the father of the two infants who'd been kidnapped for ransom. What's more, the so-called kidnap had actually been a ruse in which Mallory's wife had been complicit, designed to justify the handing over of one hundred thousand pounds from a family trust. It had all worked out well in the end, except for Mallory and Bradley.

Jack tore himself away from the salacious, and somewhat entertaining, details relating to the fraud, and concentrated on the murders in the Old Nichol, which had lain in the very centre of the area designated for the housing scheme. There had been a series of five 'unfortunate accidents' in which victims had been found dead underneath demolition rubble, and two more suspicious deaths, all of which had been linked to a man called Michael Maguire. He had been employed by Gregory Properties under a false name, notionally as a rent collector, but in reality in order to get rid of those he couldn't terrify into moving out.

The victims had all been identified and named, and none of them had been Thomas Benton. So why was there a cryptic note at the foot of his employment file indicating that he too had died in adjoining Brick Lane at approximately the same time? Who had supplied that information, and why? If it came to that, who had requested it, and again, why?

Jack was lost in speculation as the door opened and in walked Percy, while behind him lurked Blair and Pinkney.

'Sorry I'm late,' Percy apologised, 'but your aunt insisted that I deal with a malfunctioning ballcock in the outside privy. I told her that I'm a police officer, not a plumber, to which she replied, and I quote, "In this house you're a plumber, if you want any tea, and once you finally admit to being retired you'll also be a decorator, a gas fitter and a furniture restorer."'

Blair and Pinkney had been looking on with undisguised amusement while Percy had been justifying his late arrival. Jack considered that they had better things to do with their time and his, so he invited them in and asked for a progress report.

'Some of it's good, and some of it's dismal,' Blair told him as he consulted his notes. 'We can report that Herbert Gilbert's widow remarried a suspiciously short time after his suicide. Her second husband is a man she'd been conducting an affair with — it was the talk of the tenement where they were residing. According to a *very* knowledgeable old crone on the ground floor, Gilbert's suicide was more to do with his wife's carry-on with her lover.'

'So no real motivation to do away with Montague there, then,' Percy observed. 'Wasn't there something else you were supposed to be investigating?'

'Indeed there was,' Blair confirmed, 'and Claude Simpson is now employed as the warehouse manager for a fancy furniture sales firm in Mayfair. He's probably earning more than he did as a bobby.'

'Two down, but how did the last one go?' Percy asked. 'Did they give you the bum's rush?'

'The Benton business, you mean? Dead right, sir,' said Blair. 'We got absolutely nowhere when we made what we believed to be discreet enquiries in a pub called The Grapes in Nichols Square.'

'No bloody wonder!' Percy snorted. 'What they used to call the Old Nichol was at the very heart of the old slum, and Brick Lane was to one side of it. You're lucky you're still alive, if you made it known that you were investigating the murders in the Old Nichol three years ago, or mentioned Michael Maguire.'

'We didn't, sir, but that name *did* come up when we asked about a man called Thomas Benton.'

'What was said?' Jack asked eagerly.

'What was said was that Benton's death was a matter between him and his widow, and that we should "sling our hooks", which I believe is a naval term.'

'Did you think to tell them that you were police officers?' Percy asked.

'Yes, and that's when we were invited to get lost.'

'But they somehow connected Benton's death with his widow?' Jack asked.

Blair shrugged. 'I only took them to mean that since he was dead, he'd have a widow — not that she'd somehow been involved in his death.'

'Nothing more of any note from Bethnal Green?' Jack asked wearily.

'No, sorry, sir — but it was like we'd said the wrong thing. The minute we mentioned Benton, someone in the corner said, "Blame it on Maguire — he got what was coming to him for all the others, and Benton's got swept under the same carpet".'

'We never even *knew* about the death of Benton at the time,' Percy protested. 'All the others were identified and documented, but it sounds as if someone remembers Benton specifically.'

'Very well,' Jack said to Blair and Pinkney. 'Here's your next job. I want you to investigate a firm called Strand Enterprises, with an address in Essex Street in Covent Garden, just off the Strand. I want to know all about its proprietor, its line of business, its employees, and anything else you can dig up. They were the ones who provided the beer and food for the farewell ceremony at which Montague was poisoned, and the people best placed to administer that poison would have been the caterers.'

As the door closed behind Blair and Pinkney, Percy asked, 'Aren't you rather clutching at straws? Up until that dead-end report on investigations into Benton's death in Bethnal Green, you were all but convinced that someone had it in for me from the days when I put paid to Maguire and his little coterie of thugs. Now you seem to be pinning your hopes on the caterers.'

'It's not a case of one or the other,' Jack argued. 'There are two distinct issues, are there not? The first is, who would want you dead? And the second is, how would they bring it about?'

'So far as I can recall,' Percy said, 'I've always enjoyed the most cordial of relations with caterers, so why would one of them be seeking to eliminate a good customer?'

'In return for payment, clearly,' Jack replied. 'That's why I sent those two off to find out all they could about Strand Enterprises. If the business isn't doing too well financially, someone at the top might well have been tempted to add cyanide to their official menu.'

'A long shot, you have to admit,' Percy said with a frown. 'I prefer what sounded like the expressions of guilty consciences down at that pub in Nichols Square.'

'If you think so, I repeat my suggestion that you go down there in person and try applying the Enright charm,' Jack said. 'They may even remember you as the one who offered Maguire to them as a sacrificial goat.'

'Perhaps I will,' Percy murmured, 'but I won't exactly be proudly recalling my service days down there. Time for a little subterfuge, I think.'

'There's another reason why I'm interested in Strand Enterprises,' Jack revealed after a short silence. 'Do you remember how many waitresses they employed for your send-off?'

'We interviewed five altogether,' said Percy.

'That wasn't my question. Can you remember more than five?'

'No — why?'

'Well, don't tell Esther, but there was one who caught my eye while I was watching proceedings from the side, before the speech from Montague. She was in her late twenties, maybe early thirties, and had striking red hair tied up under her cap, but some of it was hanging out. Also, unusually for one of her "class", I suppose you'd say, she was wearing spectacles. She also gave me the impression that she was in charge of the rest of them, only I don't recall us interviewing her when we held all the others in the kitchen.'

'I think I remember her as well, come to think of it,' Percy said. 'She made a very pointed remark about my devotion to the chicken sandwiches, advising me that there were ham ones as well, and that some of my colleagues might like to sample the chicken. She was standing in front of the food table as if she owned it. And like you, I don't remember interviewing her afterwards.'

'She could be the key to all this!' Jack enthused. 'If we could get hold of a list of those employed by Strand Enterprises that afternoon, we could compare it with the names of those we interviewed.'

'We can do better than that,' Percy said. 'I never forget the name of a pub, and the Royal Oak in Newgate springs to mind, along with an indignant lady who was rabbiting on about being late for work there. Remember her? Lizzie something or other.'

'Lizzie Conroy,' Jack replied. 'My memory for names matches yours for pubs. Are you thinking that we should visit said pub and ask if Mrs Conroy also remembers the guardian of the chicken sandwiches?'

'Let's do that,' Percy said. 'It's coming up to dinnertime, and they might serve mutton pies and mushy peas.'

Newgate Street was the usual midday tangle and chaos of wagons, carriages, horse buses and pedestrians seemingly headed for a dozen different collision courses. Street hawkers called out their wares, newspaper vendors shouted even louder to be heard, urchins scuttled in and out in the hope of snaffling a purse or a bag, and several hopeful prostitutes lurked in the entrances to alleyways.

The interior of the Royal Oak was a scene of slowly mounting confusion as the working day began to pick up steam. It was already faintly redolent of spilled beer and hastily mopped up vomit as Jack and Percy approached the bar, behind which, brandishing a bar cloth and looking far from pleased to see them, was Lizzie Conroy.

'What d'yer want *this* time?' she grumbled.

Percy gave her one of his avuncular smiles. 'Can two gentlemen of leisure not enjoy the delights of Bowman's Best without incurring the displeasure of she who dispenses same?'

'Cut out the mealy-mouthed nonsense,' she muttered. 'Two pints o' Best, that it? It'll cost yer thruppence between yer. Let's see yer money first — we doesn't run a bleedin' charity, yer know.'

Both men savoured their first taste, and Percy wiped the foam from his lips as he asked, 'No supervisor today? They let you work unchaperoned?'

'This is the Royal Oak, not the bleedin' Lord Mayor's Banquet,' Lizzie replied indignantly. 'An' I knows me job well enough not to need a supervisor. Anyroad, the landlord's tight when it comes to employin' folks, so excuse me while I serve these other gents what's bin waitin' while yer blabber on. Enjoy yer pots, an' let me know when yer needs a refill.'

Percy waited until she'd served the two off-duty clerks from the nearby courthouse, then raised his voice in order to be heard halfway across the bar counter. 'There's obviously a world of difference between slinging out pints in an East End pub and providing proper food and drink to those who appreciate fine service.'

Jack realised what he was about, and followed suit at the same volume. 'I agree, and at your retirement party we were treated to the finest, no doubt due to the professionalism with which the event was managed.'

'If yer referrin' to that 'aughty trollop in charge of us that day, she can't've bin all that great,' came the aggrieved response as Lizzie glared at them with a reddened countenance, ''cos we ain't seen 'er since.'

'That right?' Percy asked casually, as if indifferent to her protest.

'Bloody right!' Lizzie replied forcefully. 'We 'adn't seen 'er previously, neither. "Miss Cora" she called 'erself, an' the boss said as 'ow we 'ad to take orders from 'er. She talked all fancy like, but she knew nothin' about caterin' for the gentry, that were obvious. All she did were flop around like a piece o' wet lettuce, givin' out instructions on things we knew off by 'eart anyroad. I reckon she were Mr Spencer's bit o' stuff on the side.'

'Talking of food, and recalling the day of my retirement, has made me a bit peckish,' Percy said as if he'd been ignoring her complaint. 'Do you do dinners here?'

'I can do yer bubble an' squeak for tuppence, or a plate o' whelks for the same price. The whelks is yesterday's, mind you.'

'Two portions of bubble and squeak, please,' Percy said as he handed over a sixpenny piece. 'And another pint of Best for me, if you'd be so good.'

Ten minutes later, Lizzie slid two plates of bubble and squeak across the bar counter, along with two spoons. 'So if yer retired, yer not a copper no more?' she asked Percy.

'Indeed not.'

'What about 'im?' Lizzie asked, jerking her head towards Jack.

'My day off,' Jack said, catching the warning look from Percy.

'Well, if neither of yer's a copper on duty, I'll tell yer somethin' else about that snooty Miss Cora,' Lizzie offered. 'She'd done a runner by the time we was all banged up in that kitchen. Just afore that snooty bugger keeled over, she claimed she were goin' back down to the wagon for more sandwiches, but I knew for a fact that we'd already unloaded the lot. Then when the trouble started, she were nowhere to be seen.'

'That just shows you,' Percy said ingratiatingly, 'when you've got good staff like yourself, who are so accommodating to customers, you don't need supervisors. Anyway, time for us to take our leave. You've been most helpful, and I look forward to returning to this excellent establishment in the future.'

As Jack and Percy made their way back into the bustling throng of Newgate Street, Jack said, 'You're even more insufferable when you behave like a gentleman.' He chuckled. 'And what the hell was in that bubble and squeak?'

'The squeak came from long-expired leather, to judge by the consistency of mine,' Percy replied as he pulled a face, 'but I'm now convinced that whichever of us was the target — me or Montague — the culprit was that elusive "Miss Cora". All we need to do now is find her, and I'll bet Bermondsey to a brick that she's not to be found at any future functions catered by Strand Enterprises.'

'So where next?'

'Weren't they taking photographs at my retirement do? I seem to remember the irritating flash of those bulbs that they employ.'

'Yes — well remembered!' Jack said. 'Do you want me to see if they kept any? Only, since you didn't end up retiring after all, the pictures didn't appear in the Bulletin for this month, which came out yesterday.'

'Yes, do that, please,' said Percy. 'As for me, I think I'll spend the rest of the day revisiting the scene of my alleged murder of Mangler Maguire. That way, we're keeping open both of the loose ends that we're trying to tie together.'

CHAPTER EIGHT

The memories came flooding back as Percy stepped from the warm autumn sunshine into the cool, dank front hall of Bethnal Green Police Station. He'd served two years here as a beat constable before his transfer to Scotland Yard, and he'd returned in the latter capacity three years ago in order to investigate the series of murders in the Old Nichol slum that had been immediately to the west of Brick Lane. All the victims had been tenants, or people siding with tenants, who faced eviction by Gregory Properties, the purchaser of all the properties that would shortly be demolished to make room for the planned Boundary Estate. Scotland Yard had been called in because of the seeming inability of the local force to even identify, let alone buckle, those responsible. As was normal whenever the Yard was called in over the heads of the locals, Percy had proved very unpopular.

He'd incurred the wrath of the local inspector at the time, Walter Mitchell, when he'd eventually tracked down and locked up the man behind all those murders — Michael Maguire, working under the assumed name of 'Truegood' as an enforcer for Gregory Properties. Some said that Maguire's exposure to the enraged mob that had killed him was deliberate, since it eliminated the need for a costly and uncertain trial. Inspector Mitchell had had to explain how such a lapse in security when transferring a prisoner to longer term confinement in Newgate could possibly have been allowed to occur.

Percy presented his warrant card to the desk sergeant, and received the predictable downturned mouth in exchange.

'What's the Yard doin' down 'ere?' the sergeant demanded testily.

'Nothing, until I get somewhere to sit,' Percy replied affably. 'Is your inspector still a crusty old bugger called Mitchell?'

'No, 'e retired a while back. The new man's called Tillotson, an' 'e's got no time for the Yard.'

'Then I shall seek to persuade him of the justice of my cause,' said Percy with heavy sarcasm. 'If you could let him know that I'm here in my capacity as Inspector of the Discipline Branch, I'm sure he'll be only too delighted to invite me to share a pot of tea with him.'

Twenty minutes later, Percy saw a frowning man coming down the central staircase. He introduced himself as Charles Tillotson. 'Your reputation precedes you,' Tillotson told him. 'You were the most disruptive constable this station ever had, and you caused my predecessor a good deal of grief while pretending to clean up a series of murders in the Old Nichol slums.'

'Glad to have been of service,' Percy replied. 'As you were probably told, I'm back to look into what may have been a slight dereliction of duty at that time.'

'Other than yours, you mean?'

'The curtain of charity was drawn over an unfortunate lapse in security when a prisoner was being transferred to Newgate, but I was exonerated of all blame for it anyway. Now, I'm hoping I might be afforded some temporary accommodation while I look into another death that occurred at that time, but was never actually recorded — well, at least, not properly.'

'More trouble-making?'

'No, more thorough policing. I assume that somewhere in this museum there's a file relating to the discovery of the body of one Thomas Benton, a former officer from B Division? It would have been archived at around the same time as that series of deaths in the vicinity of the former Old Nichol — Brick Lane, to be precise — and I'd like to interview the officer who filed that report. I'd also like a room made available in which to do so.'

'Anything else — a mug of tea, perhaps?' Tillotson asked.

'That would be very nice, thank you,' said Percy.

'I was told that you now head up the Discipline Branch. A case of poacher turned gamekeeper?'

'More of "set a thief to catch a thief." But I can only hope that won't prove to be the case.' Percy smiled. 'Three sugars, please.'

A further forty minutes elapsed before Percy was told, by a uniformed constable on his way out to perform his routine beat duties, that a room had been made available for him. 'It's on the top floor, next to the lavvie that's always overflowing,' said the constable.

Percy made his way to the room, dusted off the broken chair that he found behind the scratched and stained desk, and sat down, waiting for the station's wheels to crank again. More than an hour after he'd entered the station, another constable brought in a creased file that had a stain in the centre of its front cover. Clearly a mug of tea had been left on it at some time in the past.

'Better late than never,' Percy muttered, 'and I suppose that the mug of tea I ordered has been forgotten about?'

'No. We're still looking for the senna pods,' the constable replied, referring to a popular laxative.

Percy quickly realised that he was being rude, but gave him a wry smile. 'A man after my own heart. I won't do you for insubordination, because you're destined to follow the same career path as me, and that's enough punishment for anyone. Now get out.'

He read the file quickly, but it was a masterpiece of obscurity. Constable William Henderson recorded that late in the evening in question, while on patrol in Brick Lane, he'd heard the clamour of a man shouting and protesting. He'd then seen a large man and a smartly dressed woman running from an alleyway. They'd raced past him, and he'd decided to investigate. In his own words:

On reaching the doorway of the bootmaker's shop, halfway up the alleyway that was located on the right-hand side of Brick Lane, I came across the prone form of a man in his late twenties or early thirties, slumped in the doorway and seemingly bereft of life. There was a large quantity of blood emerging from what appeared to be a blow to the left side of his head, and I could not rouse him. There were several street urchins watching on, and I sent them to Bethnal Green Police Station with an account of what I had discovered, and a request for a handcart on which to transport the body. On completing this report, I went off duty at shortly after five a.m.

Mentally noting that Constable Henderson should, at that time, have remained on duty until six a.m., Percy looked in vain for a report from a physician regarding the cause of the man's death, or any account of further investigations being conducted in the immediate area among neighbours or anyone else who might have seen what had transpired. Instead, there were only a series of roughly scrawled notes by way of additions at the foot of Henderson's initial report, confirming that the deceased had died from a single blow to the head from 'a heavy implement'. In his clothing there had been several pounds in loose change, and a gold fob watch 'of considerable estimated value', bearing the inscription 'Thomas George

Benton, on his admission as a police officer, from a proud grandfather.'

Percy was able to note several significant facts arising from this later addition to the report. The first was that whatever had been the motive for the man's murder, robbery had clearly not been it. The second was that Benton's connection with the police force had obviously been established by the inscription in the fob watch, and it had to be assumed that appropriate enquiries had been made inside the Met that had enabled the authorities to identify the deceased as the man dismissed from the force some months earlier.

But several significant questions remained. Why had a man based in the West End been in one of the worst slums that the East End had to offer at that time? And why had he been earning his living as a poorly paid police constable when he obviously came from a wealthy background? Finally, why had there been no further investigation into the circumstances leading to his death? Was it simply because it had been all too easy to write him off as another of Maguire's victims? But a moment's reflection would have established that this man was not a local tenant being hounded out of his home to make way for a proposed housing development. He was a stranger to the area whose presence there required explanation, but nobody seemed to have made any effort to find out the truth.

Putting those questions aside, Percy read to the end of what was a mere two-page report, and cursed softly when he read the cryptic concluding entry, disclosing that 'the gold fob watch was released to the deceased's widow when she was able to confirm Benton's identity by way of the inscription inside the watch case.' There was no note of who the widow might have been, and no further enquiry into either her identity or her bona fides. Back when Percy had worked in Bethnal Green

Police Station, such slackness would have merited a disciplinary reprimand. It might now be long overdue, but he was determined to roast the constable responsible for such sloppy reporting and his lack of follow-up action. He would also attempt to obtain such further detail from him as he could.

He almost screamed with frustration when told by a clearly gleeful Inspector Tillotson that Constable William Henderson had resigned from the force only a matter of weeks after 'completing' his report on the death of Benton.

'Why did he resign?' Percy demanded.

Tillotson shrugged. 'No idea. I was a sergeant in Stepney at the time.'

'But it looks suspicious, does it not?'

'I don't see why. He discovered a body as part of his routine duties, then he left the force — what's suspicious about that?'

'His so-called "report" was a travesty,' Percy snorted. 'If nothing else, it was an insult to the memory of the dead man. There was no attempt to discover why — or by whom — Benton had been murdered, and a *very* obvious attempt to sweep it under the carpet when so many other bodies were turning up at that time. Speaking as one who made considerable enquiry into those deaths at the time, I recall that the other victims had multiple injuries consistent with an entire house having fallen on them. But Benton was despatched with only one blow. And I know that Benton was not included in the list supplied to me of those who had perished in the reign of terror being waged by a man named Maguire. All very strange, wouldn't you say?'

'If you say so, but none of my business,' Tillotson reminded him. 'Will you be leaving by the end of the day? Only we need your temporary office to store some stolen property.'

'In my day it would have been secured in a much safer place than a derelict third-floor office.'

'It's several barrow-loads of lead flashing from a local church,' Tillotson retorted. 'Did you have bank vaults under here in those days? And my original question remains unanswered: when do you intend to sling your hook?'

'As soon as you give me an address for the former Constable Henderson,' Percy replied.

Tillotson reached inside his tunic pocket for a folded piece of paper, which he handed over. 'See yourself out,' he said as he turned and left the office.

Sitting in the rattling, malodorous rail carriage from Shoreditch to Hackney, and recalling when he'd made the same journey back and forth each day, Percy was puzzling over the address he'd been given. Why had Constable Henderson moved to Hackney, of all places?

Percy had lived there for most of his adult life. Although he himself had begun his police career in Hackney, this was not because he'd been brought up there. His childhood and youth had been spent in rural Essex, with his parents and brother. His father had been a wealthy local doctor who had left his two sons a modest fortune on his death, two years after the death of his wife.

Percy's brother — Jack's father — had invested his inheritance in an insurance brokerage that had ensured that Jack would be born into middle-class comfort in Barking. But Percy had always been of a more egalitarian frame of mind, and was almost embarrassed to be the son of wealth. In what the family had written off as a 'mindless gesture' on Percy's part, he'd joined the police force. When allocated to his first 'home' police station in Hackney, he had purchased a house in Victoria Park Road, overlooking the spacious park of the same name. One didn't get to purchase a house in Hackney without being of at least 'comfortable' means, which made it even less explicable how a lowly constable had acquired the wherewithal to move into 17 Darnley Road, only a few streets back from where Percy lived, and one of its main commercial thoroughfares.

Consoling himself that at least he'd be able to justify an early return home after pursuing this intriguing line of enquiry, Percy alighted from the train and walked up Mare Street to its junction with Darnley Road. He soon located number 17, which was up a side alley and above a baker's shop that proudly bore the name 'Kendrick's' across its front window. He knocked on the side door, then heard footsteps descending the wooden staircase inside, before the door opened and a pleasant-faced woman asked, 'Yes? What can I do for you?'

'I'm looking for William Henderson,' Percy announced.

The woman indicated the shop entrance on the street with a wave of her hand and told him, 'You'll find Will in there. Tell him his dinner will be on the table in five minutes — that'll save me a job.'

Concluding that the house must go with whatever duties Henderson undertook inside the baker's premises, Percy thanked the woman and made his way back out into the street. He paused for a moment to examine the many tempting items on display behind the glass, then pushed open the door and savoured the smell of warm bread as he walked up to the counter and looked down at the selection of loaves, rolls, filled sandwiches and cakes. A youth who looked like an apprentice appeared behind the counter from a back room and asked, 'Yes, sir — what can I assist you with today?'

'I'm looking for Mr Henderson,' Percy announced.

'He's in the back room,' the youth replied. 'Hang on a moment.'

Henderson emerged through the doorway from the rear room, and Percy was surprised to note his apparent good health and bright smile — hardly what he'd expected to see when confronting a former beat constable from the East End.

'The boy said you wanted to see me?' said Henderson.

Percy nodded. 'It's a matter relating to your former police employment,' he replied.

'That's a few years back,' Henderson said. 'Perhaps you'd better step into my office.'

Percy did as invited and took the spare seat indicated, while Henderson perched on the edge of the chair behind his desk. Mentally noting that he was clearly apprehensive and looked as if he was about to take flight, Percy opted for a soft approach. 'I won't keep you long, since your wife says to tell you that your dinner will be on the table in five minutes.'

'But that's presumably not why you're here,' Henderson replied nervously. 'I resigned from the police force several years ago, so what's this all about? Do you have the authority to enquire into old police matters?'

Percy extracted his police badge and held it high in the air. 'What makes you think that it involves an old matter?'

'It must do, since I left the force — let me see, three years ago or more.'

'Yes, very shortly after the discovery of a body in Brick Lane,' Percy reminded him.

Henderson's smile vanished. 'It was my last case,' he replied as he cleared his throat. 'A nasty business.'

'Indeed,' Percy confirmed, 'and it's because of the perfunctory way that you compiled your report on the matter that I need to seek further details from you.'

'After three years?' Henderson replied, almost defiantly. 'There were a lot of murders in that same general area at the time, so I can hardly be expected to remember an isolated one in the series.'

'But this one wasn't down to Mangler Maguire, was it?' Percy asked, applying a little more pressure. 'Maguire's victims always resembled the aftermath of a train wreck, whereas this one — a man named Benton — had only a single blow to the head. And according to your report — brief though it was — you got a good look at two people running from the scene, a man and a woman. But no effort was made to locate them again, was it?'

'I don't recall,' Henderson said evasively. 'As I said, I left the force shortly after that, and I assume that others took over any necessary enquiries.'

'But you were still there when a lady claiming to be Benton's widow collected his gold watch, which was the means by which he was formally identified, by reference to police records. Benton was a former constable himself, was he not — stationed in Westminster?'

'He may have been — I really don't recall, and as you yourself told me, my dinner's ready, so if there's nothing else?'

At that moment, the youth appeared in the doorway with an enquiry. 'That sandwich order's ready to go off to Strand,' he told Henderson. 'Do you want to check it?'

'No, I'm happy to trust you to do that,' Henderson replied. 'Then I'm closing for dinner, so you can get off home for yours.'

'You'll be closing the shop in the middle of the day?' Percy asked. 'Does your employer condone that? You *are* the shop manager, I assume?'

'No, I'm the proprietor,' Henderson explained, visibly happier to be dealing with a question he could answer. 'I inherited the business from my grandfather on my mother's side — Samuel Kendrick. My father was dead by the time that Granddad passed away, so it came down the line to me. That's when — and why — I left the force. It was a gift horse that I couldn't possibly look in the mouth.'

'Indeed not,' Percy replied with one of his ingratiating smiles. 'And I don't suppose you'd be able to identify that widow again if you saw her?'

'The widow who claimed the gold watch? Obviously not — I only saw her twice, and the first time I just caught a fleeting glimpse.'

'As she ran past you, away from the body, you mean?' Percy said, catching him off guard.

Henderson left his chair with marked enthusiasm. He almost pushed Percy out of his way as he left the back room and re-entered the shop. 'My dinner's ready,' he said, looking back at Percy. 'Thank you for calling.'

Percy went back into the shop, purchased two meat pies and a small cob loaf, then walked back down Mare Road as far as the Crown pub. There he entered the snug and sat down in front of the elderly man reading the local weekly paper. He handed over one of the meat pies and said, 'It's been a long time again, Charlie.'

'That's your bloody fault,' the man replied. 'Gone off dominoes, have we?'

'No, there's just been a lot of pressure at work,' Percy replied. 'If I buy you a pint, can I pick your brains?'

'If you can find them,' Charlie replied.

Charlie Henstridge had been Percy's old sergeant during his first days as a beat bobby in Hackney, and had then been promoted to Inspector shortly after Percy's transfer to Bethnal Green. They'd kept in touch, and had become firm friends over twice weekly domino games in the Crown, although recently Percy's duties — and Beattie's disapproval of 'the Devil's brew' — had kept them apart. But no-one knew the history of Hackney and its residents better than old Charlie, even now, and Henderson's reference to gift horses had put Percy in mind of him.

As they sipped on their pints, Percy began, 'That bakery on Darnley Road — Kendrick's. I was in there this morning, hence the meat pies, and there seems to be a new proprietor. Did Kendrick die recently?'

'Depends on what you regard as "recent",' Charlie replied after wiping pastry from his moustache. 'Samuel Kendrick died back in the sixties.'

'That far back? But the name lived on?'

'Yes, it was still known as Kendrick's, even when the Stoppards took it over. But they never really seemed to make a go of it, mainly because Tom Stoppard drank more than he baked, to judge by the number of times I booked him into our cells. Then he went under a horse bus on the Broadway only a few years ago — his widow Clarice must have sold up.'

'Thanks, Charlie — that's given me a lot to think about,' said Percy, digesting this information. So, William Henderson had not inherited the business from his grandfather, as he'd said, but had bought it from Mrs Stoppard.

'Apart from meat pies? Is that a Kendrick's loaf under that wrapper?'

'Yes, I'm taking it home for Beattie. I only hope that the new proprietor bakes bread better than he tells lies. Another pint?'

CHAPTER NINE

Jack got home a little earlier than usual, anxious to know how Esther had fared at her interview. As he opened the front door he caught sight of her beaming face, and before he could even remove his coat she rushed down the hallway, threw her arms around him and announced, 'I got accepted — and I start next Monday!'

'That's wonderful!' Jack enthused between kisses. 'But what about your work at the school? And won't you need to make arrangements for someone to take Bertie and Lily to school and back every day?'

'That's already organised,' Esther assured him breathlessly. 'The classes don't start until nine in the morning, and the bus only takes ten minutes or so, since East Ham's only down the road from here. So I can walk the children to school, then catch the horse bus that leaves every twenty minutes, including one at eight-forty that will get me there in time for classes, and Alice has agreed to pick them up in the afternoons. It's only for a month, anyway, since the *lovely* woman who runs the course I'll be taking says that I need only do four weeks, and if all goes well she'll give me my accreditation. I think I quite impressed her at my interview, when I put the other two old fogeys in their places!'

Jack chuckled. 'I can well imagine. Did they ask the predictable question that we practised your answer for — the one about whether or not your husband approved of your ambition?'

'It was the very first question, and I felt *so* proud to be able to reply that we agree on everything in our life together. Then it was suggested that I'd be abandoning the children, and I batted that one back smartly by telling him that we had servants for that sort of thing. I think that knocked the two men on the interviewing panel sideways, particularly when I managed to slip in the additional fact that you're a senior Scotland Yard officer on a generous salary.'

'Sounds as if you had a very triumphant day,' Jack said. 'May I take my coat off now?'

'Of course, and on my way home I stopped at the butcher's and got you your favourite lamb chops, just to say thank you for being so — so — well, so *you*, I suppose.'

'It comes naturally,' Jack said with a grin. 'But won't you be leaving the local school in the lurch if you start down the road next Monday?'

'That's all sorted as well. Miss Allsop, who's the principal of the college, and who was the one leading the interview, assures me that she can supply someone from the college to replace me, although it seems that it'll be someone without any practical experience.'

'And what about the teaching hours that you need to clock up before qualifying for the course?'

'I've got enough under my belt already, it seems. So everything's just worked out perfectly, and I'm *so* happy!'

'I'd never have guessed,' Jack said with a laugh. 'Have you told the children yet?'

'Yes, although I'm not sure that they fully understand. When I told Bertie that he and Lily would be walked home by Alice, he proved himself to be a chip off the old block by attempting to bargain with me.'

'Oh? What did he say?'

'Apparently the local militia regiment — I believe that their official title is "The Volunteer Battalion of the Essex

Regiment", or something like that — are marching through Barking on Saturday, from the railway station to the old abbey ruins, and Bertie wants to go and watch them. You know how fascinated he is by anything to do with soldiers. He saw his opportunity when he sensed that I needed his co-operation for the new arrangement with Alice. You have to admire his intelligence for a boy of five. So can we go and watch them?'

'Of course, but what does Lily want in exchange?'

'Nothing, so far as I'm aware. She just said, "Yes, Mummy," like the sweet child that she is. Miriam and Tommy won't notice any difference, since Alice looks after them all day anyway. But while she's off to collect Bertie and Lily from school, Polly will need to keep an eye on them. Miriam always seems interested in what goes on in the kitchen anyway.'

'And what reward do I get for being the compliant husband?'

'Wait until bedtime. And now let's go and treat ourselves to a celebration sherry, shall we?'

The following morning, Percy breezed into Jack's office with a broad grin and took the seat in front of his desk.

'Esther's got herself onto that teacher training course,' Jack told him, 'and you look almost as happy as her. What are you so chipper about?'

'Wait until I tell you what I found out yesterday, while making a nuisance of myself down in Bethnal Green.'

'I imagine that was enough in itself to make your day,' Jack said, 'but I've got a mountain of paperwork in front of me, so give me the short version.'

'I think I know how Thomas Benton got murdered, and who by!'

'That sounds like a good return on a day's enquiries. Please enlighten me.'

'The discovery of the body was allegedly made by a Constable William Henderson, who immediately prior to that discovery heard a man shouting, then saw two people — a man and a woman — running down Brick Lane. The deceased had just one head wound — a single blow from a heavy implement, unlike all Maguire's victims, who ended up looking like raw meat on a butcher's slab. And the motive for his murder obviously wasn't robbery, because he was still carrying some loose change and a *very* valuable gold fob watch inscribed with his name. That's how they learned who he was, but the subsequent reporting on the file was abysmal — so bad as to be suspicious, in fact. But the new inspector down there was playing it down, probably because it reflects badly on his station, even though he wasn't the inspector at the time.'

'I *do* have other things to do,' Jack reminded him tersely. 'Come on, I'm yawning with anticipation.'

'Constable Henderson resigned from the force shortly after Benton's murder, giving an address in Hackney.'

Jack frowned. 'How did a beat constable afford a house in Hackney? From what I remember of my formative days there, living with you and Aunt Beattie, you need a small fortune to buy into Hackney, or at least you did in those days. You used your legacy from Grandfather, as I recall — or did you rob a bank?'

'For someone who claims to have a lot to do, you've got a lot to say for yourself — do you want the next gem or not?'

'You traced Henderson to his new lair in Hackney?'

'I did indeed. Do you remember Kendrick's Bakery in Darnley Road?'

'Enough to recall the taste of their stale buns. Why?'

'Well, Henderson told me that he's now its proprietor: he said he inherited it from his grandfather, a Kendrick on his mother's side. But — and hold onto your hat — further enquiries by me with someone who knows the history of Hackney revealed that old Kendrick died some thirty years ago. The business was sold to a family named Stoppard, and was resold only three years or so ago — to Henderson, presumably.'

'And so we naturally have to ask ourselves where he got the money from?'

'Precisely. The smell of bribery is hanging in the air. But there's something else — something that set my teeth on edge.'

'I've already decided that this paperwork on my desk can wait until after dinner, so please continue,' Jack urged him.

'The matter of the gold watch, which was handed to a woman claiming to be Benton's widow with only the most perfunctory of enquiries regarding her bona fides. Henderson, in his report, tried to justify that by asserting that it helped to confirm the victim's true identity, although by then it was no longer possible to have the grieving lady view the remains.'

'And?'

'*And*, when I asked Henderson if he could identify the lady in question, he dropped his guard. How someone that stupid ever got into the Met is beyond me.'

'Get *on* with it!' Jack snapped.

Percy smiled. 'His answer was that he'd only seen her twice, and the first time had been only a fleeting glimpse!'

Jack thought for a moment, then the penny dropped. 'The first time being when she rushed down Brick Lane in the company of a man!'

'Precisely! When I put that suggestion to him, he departed with the speed of a thousand spooked horses.'

'So let's think through the implications,' Jack mused. 'Benton's so-called widow was present at his death, and may well have organised it by luring him down the alleyway, given that Bethnal Green was not a place he was familiar with, and he was no longer a serving police officer. Then she turns up again to claim the gold watch, either because it's valuable, or because it will give away Benton's identity, although unknown to her it already has. Then Henderson takes a massive bribe to keep his mouth shut about having seen the alleged widow at the scene of the murder.'

'My conclusions exactly, Jack my boy. So my day wasn't exactly wasted.'

'I still have two questions,' Jack objected. 'First, what possible connection could there be between the murder of Benton, possibly by, or with the connivance of, his widow, and the murder of Chief Superintendent Montague, either intentionally or because the poison was meant for you?'

'No idea — yet. But I intend to find out.'

'Which leads to my second question. What's the connection between this mysterious woman claiming to be Benton's widow and the caterers, who may have hired a poisoner?'

'Again, I intend to find out, when our two hired bloodhounds return with further information relating to Strand Enterprises. Nothing new there, I assume?'

'No, but if you're thinking along the same lines as me, you'll be hoping that Benton's widow is our missing waitress from the farewell party.'

'I obviously taught you well,' Percy said. 'And there's something else I forgot to mention. While I was chatting away to Henderson, his shop assistant revealed that they were about to send a load of sandwiches off to "Strand". Could that be Strand Enterprises, do we think? Does Henderson have an ongoing supply contract with the very same firm that supplied the poison, or so we believe?'

'You taught me well enough to exercise caution when assuming that the poisoning — whoever might have been the intended victim — had anything to do with the death of Benton, other than the fact that he was thrown off the force by Montague. A woman who's capable of organising the murder of her husband would be unlikely to be seeking revenge against the man who gave him his marching orders from the Met. It's not as if he thereby suffered the loss of a valuable income. But, by the same token, how did he come to be in possession of a gold watch?'

'A gift from his grandfather, apparently, according to the inscription inside it.'

'So he *came* from money? A bit like me?'

'To an extent, but to the best of my knowledge you didn't sexually assault female prisoners, so the similarity only goes so far.'

'But we still haven't managed to join one end of the string to the other, have we? We have a murder in Bethnal Green at one end, and the poisoning of a senior police officer at the other. Where's the connection?'

'We won't know until we join the ends, either by working from the middle outwards, or by learning that the same woman was involved in both cases.'

'So where do we go next?'

'Not "we", Jack — me. I'm proposing that I go back into Bethnal Green, but this time as a casual visitor to one or more of its pestilential alehouses.'

'Where, as you once commented, you'll be as welcome as a bowl of bubonic plague.'

'As Detective Inspector Enright, certainly. But I recently retired, did I not?'

'Officially you did, yes. Presumably your idea is to pose as a recently retired bobby who retains a morbid interest in a three-year-old murder? I don't fancy your chances.'

'Oh ye of little faith, Jackson, as your mother insisted on calling you. Your sister Lucy isn't the only one given to pretending to be someone else.'

'Let me at least buy you a last supper,' Jack suggested. 'It's not even midday yet, but I can't face all these application forms on an empty stomach, and I hear the call of Tan Li's.'

Everyone was struck dumb when Percy walked into the Well and Bucket on Bethnal Green Road shortly after eight o'clock that evening, and perched on a vacant stool at the bar. The hush that had descended on the large gathering of labourers, resident drunks and transient ne'er-do-wells would be useful for what he had in mind, but it looked as if he might have to wait a while for a drink.

'We doesn't serve rozzers,' the burly man behind the bar announced down his twice broken nose.

'Then I obviously retired just in time,' Percy replied, 'and mine's a pint of your best, if you'd be so good.'

He then turned to those who were staring at him, apparently stunned that he had either the courage, or the stupidity, to walk into this particular den of depravity when he was known to just about everyone in there, and not in a good way.

'You didn't hear incorrectly, gentlemen. I am indeed retired, and am now happily engaged in my new career as a private investigator, or "enquiry agent", as I prefer to call myself. And in that capacity, I've recently been engaged by a wealthy family from Westminster to locate those entitled to inherit under a trust fund established many years ago for the descendants of one Tobias Benton, a leather merchant based in Mayfair. I need not descend into the detail of what transpired as the years passed, but suffice it to say that the last-known person to become the beneficiary of a trust fund that now extends to several thousand pounds was a man called Thomas Benton, who died tragically just around the corner from here three years ago. He is believed to have left a widow, and perhaps several children, but my clients, the trustees of the trust, cannot be certain of that, since he had been estranged from the family ever since he renounced his opportunity to join the family business — a retail store in the West End. So the reason for my visit here this evening is to enquire whether or not any of you can put me in contact with either Benton's widow, or some other member of his family. I might add that I am authorised to part with the sum of one hundred pounds to anyone who can supply information that will reveal the identity and whereabouts of any known surviving relatives of Thomas Benton.'

'That'll be tuppence,' the man behind the bar announced as he placed a foaming pot on the counter. 'Everyone else pays a penny 'alfpenny, but rozzers gets to pay that bit extra.'

'Then I shall expect a halfpenny change,' Percy said as he slid two pence across the wet ale spillage on the counter, then turned back to address the still silent crowd. 'May I take it that either no-one has any knowledge of any widow or child of the late Thomas Benton, or — if they have — that they have no immediate need for a hundred pounds?'

'This another o' yer tricks, Enright?' demanded a scrawny man propped against a well-abused piano in the corner. 'If yer not a rozzer no more, yer musta bin chucked out.'

'I recently retired from the force by way of a very respectful party held in my honour,' Percy replied. 'They presented me with a carriage clock that is now in pride of place on my mantelpiece at home.'

''Ow can yer be sure that Benton's widow didn't do the man in 'erself?' asked another man covered in what looked like coal dust.

'I can't, obviously,' Percy replied, 'but if that's what happened, then my clients would be *very* pleased to learn of that fact. Can you confirm it, and what evidence do you have for that very bold assertion?'

It fell quiet, apart from a few furtive mutterings among a group of labourers further down the bar counter, one of whom looked up and asked, 'Yer sayin' as 'ow Cora might be entitled to money, if she didn't do 'er 'usband in?'

'Cora? Is that her name?' Percy asked. 'If so, where might I find her?'

'I'll show yer,' the same man offered as he drew himself up to his full six feet. 'Foller me.'

Percy finished his pint, made a gesture of prising his halfpenny change from the sticky bar counter and dropping it in the 'poor box' that almost certainly supplemented the barkeeper's meagre wage, then followed the broad-shouldered man out of the bar and into the street. He was obliged to hurry in order to match the man's swift strides as they turned out of Bethnal Green Road and into Chandler's Court, where the only light was coming from a window above an ironmonger's premises. The man stopped abruptly and turned, revealing a massive bricklayer's hammer that had been concealed in his heavy overcoat. Percy turned quickly, seeking a means of escape, only to realise that they had been followed, and that a man of equal size to the one he'd been following was blocking his exit from the narrow alley.

'Yer made a big mistake in there, rozzer,' the man with the hammer snarled as he took two steps towards Percy with the hammer raised to shoulder height. 'If yer was *really* 'ired by the family of 'im what died, then yer woulda known that 'is widow were called Cora. But them what made it possible to cover up 'ow she came to be a widow don't take kindly to yer stickin' yer toffee nose inter matters what don't concern yer. Cora missed yer last time, but I won't. Everyone 'eard as 'ow yer got a century 'idden away in that fancy waistcoat, so when they find yer body, they'll just think yer was rolled for that.'

'I have something else as well,' Percy replied coolly, inwardly cursing that he was now obliged to abandon his cover story as he extracted the revolver from inside his bulky overcoat. 'Who's first?'

CHAPTER TEN

The following morning, Jack sighed as he contemplated the mounting pile of application forms from would-be recruits who he was required to interview whenever he got the opportunity, then looked up when he sensed a presence in his doorway. It proved to be the uniformed constable who ran errands for Assistant Commissioner Bruce, and he looked far from friendly.

'The AC wants to see you — now, or in ten seconds with your arms up your back. Your choice — sir.'

Jack was barely inside Bruce's office when the Assistant Commissioner bellowed, 'What the hell did Enright think he was up to last night?'

'You mean my uncle?' Jack asked, without thinking.

'Of *course* I mean your uncle — are there any other Enrights on the force that I have to contend with?'

'What's he done?' Jack asked as he anticipated the worst.

'He's currently in the process of being released from Bethnal Green Police Station on my authority, after being run in for shooting two men, *that's* what he's done. One of them's dead, and the other won't be walking for a considerable period, if at all. You were given a specific order that *you* were leading the enquiry into the poisoning of Chief Superintendent Montague, and yet it would seem that you let your uncle run riot through the East End without attempting to supervise what he was about. Can you claim otherwise?'

'No,' Jack admitted feebly. 'But from what you tell me, may I conclude that he came to no harm? I'm sure he had a very good reason for his actions, and was forced to shoot in self-defence.'

'No doubt, but what I need to know is what in God's name he was doing that required him to take such drastic action?'

'There have been significant developments in our enquiries, sir,' Jack began to explain. 'First of all, we believe that the real target for the poisoning may have been my uncle. Secondly, we believe that the unexplained murder of a former officer in B Division who was dismissed from the force by Montague may be attributed to his widow, and that she's somehow linked with the poisoning attempt. It also may relate back to a former case that was investigated — successfully — by Inspector Enright.'

'If she was in some way seeking revenge against Enright, then why was Montague the one who was poisoned?'

'We believe that the perpetrator may have poisoned the wrong beer glass.'

'When you say "we", can you assure me that you still have control of this matter, and haven't just let your uncle take over the show, playing by his own set of rules, which rarely coincide with the Procedures Manual?'

'Absolutely, sir.'

'That's perhaps as well, because Enright was told, on his release, that he's no longer a serving Met officer. His delayed retirement has been revoked. He's to be allowed nowhere near this matter in future, understood?'

'Yes, sir. What about Sergeant Blair and Constable Pinkney, sir?'

'They will remain at your disposal until the end of the day, after which they're being transferred to Armed Robberies. Then you're on your own.'

'Yes, sir,' Jack nodded with resignation as he turned to go.

'Stay there — I haven't finished yet!' Bruce snapped, and Jack braced himself for more. 'I'm advised,' Bruce continued tersely, 'that there is a mounting backlog of applicants awaiting final interview for acceptance into the Met. You were appointed in the first place because it was believed that you could improve recruitment numbers, but in fact those numbers have fallen alarmingly since you took over your new office. There are even rumours that potential recruits are being put off by tales that the process takes forever. See to it, if you wish to keep your exalted rank. And don't blame your lack of progress on the investigation into Montague's death. You should be capable of discharging both sets of duties at once. So don't hang about, looking like a seagull on a wall. Get *on* with it, before I think of something worse to say!'

Back in his office, Jack was still muttering under his breath as he reached reluctantly for the pile of potential interview candidates with a view to passing some of the work down to the sergeant beneath him. Sergeant Blackwell had so far not been called upon to substitute for him, and was no doubt the one who had tipped off Bruce regarding the growing backlog. Jack looked up with an irritated tut as Blair and Pinkney first darkened his doorway, then stepped inside his office.

'I gather that you're only assigned to me until the end of today,' Jack said wearily, 'so what have you got for me on Strand Enterprises?'

'Sweet bugger all, sir, I'm afraid,' Blair admitted. 'They don't exist.'

'What?' Jack said. 'They *must* exist — they were the ones who handled the catering for the do at which Montague was poisoned!'

'They exist in a physical sense, obviously, sir,' Blair conceded. 'They have two rooms above a bookshop on Essex Street, and they do indeed conduct an external catering business, but there's no paperwork on them in the Companies Office.'

'Perhaps it's a partnership or something, then,' Jack suggested. 'Or even a one-man show. Have you got nothing on them at all?'

'Not officially, sir, but we made enquiries with F Division, which covers Essex Street. All they could tell us was that the business is above board, has not been reported for any disorder or dishonesty, and only comes to the attention of the beat bobbies when its wagons cause an occasional blockage in the street while loading in the course of their business. The proprietor's name is apparently Spencer, and he's highly thought of by various local charities to whom he donates leftover food when appropriate.'

'Hmm, very well,' Jack replied. 'Go down to Chief Superintendent Montague's former office and get me all the paperwork you can on the preparations for the farewell party that was the occasion of his death. Presumably the catering was tendered for, and there may be more to be learned about Strand Enterprises from that process. Then I think that will just about conclude your duties working alongside me. Thank you for all your enquiries.'

'At least we weren't being shot at while we carried them out,' Pinkney muttered as they turned to leave, 'which is more than can be said about our next posting.'

Once they'd left, Jack called out for Sergeant Blackwell, who occupied a desk in a corridor alcove alongside Jack's office. He came in, and Jack slid two lists of names across the desk towards him.

'Those marked "E" are to be interviewed by me, starting next Tuesday, while the "B" list is yours. You can use one of the witness interview rooms on the ground floor. Your list is considerably longer than mine, which should leave you with little time to nip upstairs and peach on me to the Assistant Commissioner.'

Blackwell gave him a pained look, took the list, and walked back out, almost colliding in the doorway with a constable from the front desk. The constable entered the office and dropped a single sheet of paper onto Jack's desk. 'It were left at the front door, sir. It's addressed to you, as yer can see.'

Jack thanked him and opened it, hardly surprised to learn that the note came from Percy, and simply read, *Tan Li's — twelve noon — my treat.*

'Glad to see that I'm still alive?' Percy asked with a grin as Jack slid into the seat opposite his at the small table to the rear of the already busy chophouse. 'Your face rather indicates the contrary.'

'You dropped me right in it!' Jack complained. 'What were you thinking?'

'I was learning much more in connection with our joint investigation,' Percy said. 'You can thank me now or in ten seconds' time.'

'All I can thank you for at present is the fact that I'm now completely on my own in what you choose to call our "joint" investigation,' Jack retorted. 'Meanwhile, I'm also trying to catch up with my actual job, which I'm in imminent danger of losing due to the distraction of the Montague business. I'm on my own because as a consequence of you firing that revolver you had no business retaining after your official retirement. And of course you're now out of the Yard completely.'

'Not that I have the slightest intention of letting that slow me down,' Percy assured him. 'No-one sets out to poison me and gets away with it.'

'We still don't know for sure that you were the target,' Jack reminded him.

'We do now, thanks to the information I obtained last night.'

'At gunpoint?'

'No, that came later. Now, let's order first, then I'll tell you what I learned before two thugs tried to do me in.'

'This had better be good, or I'll tip whatever you order all over your head.'

Just then, a waiter took their order then shuffled back towards the kitchen door, out of earshot.

'Well,' Percy began, 'I took myself down to the lowest drinking den in Bethnal Green and pretended that after my retirement I'd become a private enquiry agent. I said I was looking for relatives of Thomas Benton because they were due to inherit his portion of a substantial family trust, and that there were a hundred big ones in it for anyone who could supply the necessary information. I rapidly learned that the widow who we believe was involved in his death is called Cora. That was my big mistake, as it turns out, since I unthinkingly let it be known that I hadn't been aware of her name up until that point. If I'd been instructed by the trustees, as I pretended I had been, I would have known that.'

'And that's when it turned ugly?'

'Both ugly *and* productive.' Percy nodded towards a waiter who was making his way to their table, carrying a plate of pork. 'This looks like yours — mine's presumably still grazing in a field somewhere in Surrey.'

'I'm about to earn this,' Jack said as he took his first mouthful. 'You said that the alleged widow's name was Cora, yes?'

'That's right,' Percy confirmed as his beef steak was delivered and he picked up his knife and fork.

'Then she has the same name as the woman in charge of the waitresses at your farewell do. If you recall, the *delightful* Lizzie Conroy, the barmaid at the Royal Oak, was able to recall a "Miss Cora", whose supervisory skills were lacking. Lizzie put her lack of experience down to the possibility that she was in some sort of relationship with Mr Spencer, the proprietor of Strand Enterprises. But it could be that she took the job in order to poison someone — perhaps Montague, but I now think it's more likely that you *were* the intended target. So why have you become more drawn to the same conclusion?'

'Because of something the blighter who came at me with a hammer said — the same man who did for Benton, at a guess, since he seemed to know a lot about how he came to die, and the cause of Benton's death was a blow to the head with a heavy implement. His name was George Mulherron, by the way — you might want to look into his past.'

'He was the one you shot dead?'

'The very same. The man I shot in the backside, or somewhere fairly close, when he tried to flee the scene is called Walter Jamieson. You might wish to scour Criminal Records for him as well.'

Jack jotted both names down in his notebook, then looked enquiringly back at Percy. 'Well, what did he say that made you think that you were the target at the farewell do?'

'His exact words, as I recall them, were "Cora missed you last time, but I won't." He also said something about someone covering up how she became a widow in the first place, which makes me think that she was indeed complicit in the murder of her husband.'

'So the recent attack on you — and the bungled poisoning — was some sort of attempt to prevent you investigating Cora's involvement in her husband's murder?'

'All this food is obviously interfering with your reasoning processes,' Percy observed. 'We had no occasion to look into the death of Thomas Benton until the failed poisoning, did we? So the recent attack on me must have been solely because I was getting too close to Benton's murder, which raises the intriguing question of what I've done in the past to merit being poisoned by Cora in the first place.'

'Or someone on whose behalf Cora was acting? If it's connected with those original Bethnal Green murders, then the only people seeking revenge against you must be the relatives of Maguire.'

'Assuming he had any,' said Percy. 'And if he did, I probably did them a favour, if they're honest with themselves. So we're almost back where we started.'

'You mean *I* am, thanks to you,' Jack said with a frown. 'How do you intend to continue to assist me now you're officially retired from the force?'

'We have to find some other way of meeting. The comfort of this seat and the quality of this steak gives me a good idea.'

'And too much food will likely to give *me* indigestion and a waistline like yours,' Jack objected, 'so think again.'

'Don't imagine that I haven't,' Percy said. 'Does Polly still do a good lamb roast?'

'Are you thinking of reviving the old Sunday lunch tradition, without the handicap of Mother insisting that we don't talk shop?'

'I've always maintained that you're quick on the uptake,' Percy said. 'Make sure that Lucy and Teddy are invited as well — we can begin this coming Sunday.'

'Esther starts her new teaching course the following day,' Jack objected, 'so she's hardly likely to want the distraction of playing hostess. And why Lucy and Teddy?'

'Well, Lucy really. We need to find out more about what goes on inside that catering outfit that does poisoning on demand.'

'Strand Enterprises? I learned only this morning that they don't exist in the registers at the Companies Office, and that the proprietor — Mr Spencer — is well regarded by the local force based in Bow Street.'

'All the more reason why we need someone to go in undercover and learn more. Esther left me in no doubt that she won't play my games anymore, so we have to make use of another Enright resource.'

Jack chuckled. 'Good luck with that. The last time you dragged Lucy into one of our investigations, you insisted that she dress up as a ghost in a railway station waiting room. And that was a few years ago now.'

'Well, it's worth a try, anyway. And if I can't persuade you to join me here for the remaining two days of this week, then I'll see you on Sunday.'

'I take it that you're not attending the memorial service for Montague on Friday?'

Percy sighed. 'I suppose I should, given that he drank the poison intended for me. But somehow I doubt that my attendance would be welcomed by a certain Assistant Commissioner.'

'All right, I'll order the lamb roast for Sunday when I get home,' Jack conceded. 'Any other requests?'

'Yes — don't let on to your Aunt Beattie that I'm no longer officially a rozzer.'

When Jack returned from his lunch with Percy, he found an envelope lying on his desk, inside which were several photographs of the fatal farewell ceremony. He found a suitable one and nodded with satisfaction at the clarity with which it displayed the countenance of the very attractive, but completely out of place, "Miss Cora". He put it inside his jacket, hoping that Esther wouldn't find it and draw the wrong conclusion.

When he got home and told Esther about the planned Sunday lunch, he anticipated a vigorous protest. He was therefore pleasantly surprised by her smiling response.

'I love those family get-togethers, when we can catch up with Lucy and Teddy — and Percy and Beattie, of course, although I imagine that you two will talk shop all afternoon,' she said. 'As if you don't get the opportunity to do that every day at work. And having to play hostess will take my mind off Monday morning. As will Saturday, of course.'

'What are you doing on Saturday?'

'*Us*, dear — remember that we promised Bertie that he could go and watch the local soldiers parading their flag?'

'I hadn't forgotten,' Jack lied as he suppressed a sigh. 'I was just making sure that you hadn't.'

The following day was a comparably quiet one, so after signing off on the order of candidate interviews for the following Tuesday, Jack sent Sergeant Blackwell down to Criminal Records to gather whatever information might be available on the late George Mulherron and the injured Walter Jamieson, Percy's two attackers.

The local community in Bethnal Green was well rid of George Mulherron, Jack concluded, as he read his dismal career history as a 'standover merchant' for various persons of ill repute in the same locality — in the main, pawnbrokers and moneylenders. He'd also been interviewed, although not by Percy apparently, in connection with the original Maguire murders. He had managed to convince some idiot on the local force that he'd been at home in bed during each of them. As for Walter Jamieson, his budding career as a housebreaker would no doubt suffer a significant downturn due to his current injury. There was nothing worth following up on for either of them, but Percy would no doubt be gratified to learn that he hadn't shot any local citizens of worth.

Friday was almost entirely absorbed by the memorial service for the late Chief Superintendent Herbert Montague, which by the tradition established for officers who'd fallen in the course of duty was held inside Westminster Abbey. Jack had hoped to avoid Assistant Commissioner Bruce, but he wasn't quite quick enough when filing out of the gloomy cavern of England's finest cathedral. He felt a heavy hand on his uniformed shoulder just as he stepped out into the autumn sunlight.

'There you are, Enright,' said Bruce. 'Delighted to hear that you're making progress on those recruitment interviews. Next week, isn't it?'

'Yes, sir,' Jack replied. 'Sergeant Blackwell was quite correct.'

On Saturday he witnessed pomp and ceremony of a different sort, as the Volunteer Battalion of the Essex Regiment, complete with band, formed up outside the railway station. On the given command, the band struck up with 'The British Grenadiers' and the columns moved off from the station forecourt into the main street. The choice of tune, although very popular with military bands, was slightly inappropriate, given that the Essex Regiment was an infantry regiment rather than artillery. But nothing marred the pride of those keeping time as the columns swung right towards the back street that would turn into the country lane in which the Enrights were waiting to view their progress towards the old abbey ruins.

The men were all, as their battalion name implied, volunteers, and not part of the full-time armed force that Britain kept on standby in case of threats of foreign aggression.

Apart from several intense skirmishes in South Africa that had been reported in the newspapers, there had been no major wars in recent years. As a result, the number of men volunteering to engage in weekend exercises in return for a few shillings, with no immediate risk of encountering any enemy, had grown considerably in recent years.

Bertie insisted that Jack lift him onto his broad shoulders as the column came closer to their vantage point. He then cheered at the top of his voice as the khaki-clad weekend warriors kicked up the dust from the lane. When they'd disappeared from sight, and Esther was gathering their remaining children ahead of the walk back to Church Lane, Jack asked Bertie why he was so fascinated by soldiers.

'They get to kill people, don't they?' he enthused.

'Yes, but that's not a good thing,' Jack replied, somewhat alarmed.

'They have guns, though,' said Bertie. 'Why do they get guns if killing is bad?'

'It depends on who they shoot with them,' Jack reasoned.

'Bad people?'

'Yes, bad people.'

'Do *you* have a gun to shoot bad people?'

'Sometimes.'

'And have you ever shot a bad person?'

'Just once,' Jack admitted, as he recalled how he'd saved Percy's life from under a wagon in a pub yard in Plaistow.

'But not this week?'

'No, not this week,' Jack confirmed, as he remembered that Percy had indeed fired his gun recently.

CHAPTER ELEVEN

'The guests will be here in little more than an hour,' Esther reminded Jack on Sunday morning as he sat at the dining table, on which he'd spread out half a dozen pieces of paper, 'and you're still in your pyjamas and dressing gown.'

'It's not as if we're expecting the Queen or the Lord Mayor of London,' Jack replied. 'It's only family, and they've seen me like this before.'

'Not since before we met, and only at various stages of your childhood and early youth. In any case, Alice will need to set the dining table before supervising the children's lunch in the kitchen. What have you got there, anyway?'

'Various documents in connection with the case that Percy and I are working on,' he told her. 'I need to make sense of them before he arrives.'

Esther tutted. 'You've got every working day to do that, so why is it so important to have them assessed by lunchtime today?'

'It just is,' Jack replied unhelpfully, 'and I'm almost finished.'

The conclusion he'd tentatively reached, while confirming a suspicion, was nevertheless startling. Spread out before him were the documents relating to the tender process conducted in preparation for Percy's farewell ceremony that Blair and Pinkney had delivered on Friday afternoon, prior to bidding him a final farewell. In strict accordance with how things were accounted for in the Met, the 'Expressions of Interest' document that had sought tenders for Percy's retirement ceremony had called for a 'price per head' estimate from those external caterers who cared to bid for the work. They had been required to provide a finger buffet of sandwiches, savoury pastries and cakes, and an estimated twenty gallons or thereby of mid-range beer.

There had been five written estimates in response, four of which had exceeded ten shillings per head, and a bid from Strand Enterprises that quoted six. The disparity was so huge that Jack had been carefully perusing the detailed specifications supplied by each bidder as part of their tenders, to ensure that they were comparable, and with minor deviations they were. The evidence was undeniable — Strand had severely undercut the competition.

There could be several reasons for this. The first was the obvious one — that whoever was in charge at Strand Enterprises was seriously incompetent. Another was that they were prepared to run on a tight profit margin, or even incur a marginal loss, in order to be able to add the event to their portfolio to attract future clients. In addition, of course, someone within the Yard could have leaked details of the other bids to Strand Enterprises, but if so, one would have expected their bid to be higher than it was. The final possibility was that Strand Enterprises wished to ensure that they were the ones chosen to cater for the event, given that they knew that Percy would be the guest of honour, and that it would provide them with the perfect opportunity to poison him.

Jack was appropriately dressed when Percy and Beattie arrived, the latter with a face as stiff as a flat iron. They'd barely removed their outdoor clothing when Beattie turned to Jack and said, 'Perhaps you can tell me why your uncle seems unwilling to explain why he didn't return home on Wednesday night, leaving me fearful that something awful had happened to him.'

Percy shot Jack a pleading look, and Jack replied, 'I'm sure that Uncle Percy explained that our enquiries took us back to Bethnal Green, and needed to be conducted under the cover of darkness.'

The intense look of relief on Percy's face confirmed that Jack had managed an explanation vaguely consistent with whatever cock-and-bull story Percy had fed his wife to conceal the fact that he'd spent the night in the Bethnal Green police cells. Beattie responded with a non-committal grunt as she progressed towards the living room and the sherry decanter that Esther would no doubt be wielding.

'Well done, boy,' Percy muttered as he passed Jack in the hall a few paces behind Beattie.

Jack just had time to insist, 'I'm not a boy anymore,' when the front door chimes sounded again, and he headed towards them in order to welcome Lucy, Teddy and their brood.

'So tomorrow's your big day,' Lucy said to Esther over sherry. 'Are you feeling nervous?'

'I'm not sure whether the butterflies in my stomach are those of apprehension or happy anticipation, but tomorrow certainly marks a big step forward in my career as a teacher,' Esther replied.

'Not that she needs one, of course,' Beattie observed drily. 'Given Jack's exalted rank there's obviously no call for any additional income, but perhaps, like me, she needs something to occupy those lonely hours when the breadwinner is out on the streets, exposing himself to danger, and one never knows when he's coming home — or indeed *if*.'

'*We* have some exciting news as well,' Lucy announced before Beattie could travel any further on her hobby horse. 'Teddy's architectural firm will be combining with a London-wide building contractor in a new venture to provide housing for people of quality along that outer northern strip that's still underdeveloped — Marylebone, Camden, and all the way out to Harrow.'

'Will you be having a celebration party?' Percy asked, with a sly glance at Jack.

'Typical Percy!' Beattie said with a snort. 'Such a wonderful opportunity for his niece and her husband, and all he can focus on is the prospect of food! And if my nose doesn't deceive me, and we're having a lamb roast for lunch, you can guarantee that I'll be letting out the waistband of his trousers — *again* — before he can wear them to work tomorrow.'

Beattie was proved right when fifteen minutes later a massive leg of lamb was placed in the centre of the table by Polly, while Alice followed with dishes of vegetables. Jack stood up and began carving the meat onto dinner plates that were passed down the table as Teddy picked up the earlier conversation.

'Beattie mentioned your work, Percy, and so I take that as permission to follow up on the theme. Has there been any progress on that ugly poisoning business?'

Percy nodded. 'Considerable, as it happens. The first thing I can disclose is that Esther was correct, and the intended target was almost certainly me. Such evidence as we've been able to garner at this stage suggests that someone out there wanted to pay me back for something I did during my years in the Met. Unfortunately, I banged away so many villains during those years that we're spoiled for choice.'

'But you would surely have recognised anyone attending the farewell party who you'd put away in the past?' Teddy asked.

'Obviously, which is why our primary suspects are now the caterers,' said Jack. 'It would have been all too easy for them to slip someone into the waitress team armed with the appropriate amount of cyanide hidden in her apron pocket.

119

Which reminds me, Uncle Percy — after you left the office yesterday, we got those photographs from the ceremony. In this one, you can clearly see the lady we recall as having been in charge of the waitresses supplied by the catering company — "Miss Cora", she called herself, if you remember.'

He slipped the photograph from inside his jacket and passed it across the table to Percy, who frowned and leaned forward to get a closer look.

'I didn't realise it at the time — mainly because I was too busy avoiding small talk with senior officers while ensuring that I got enough to eat — but that young woman's face is familiar to me.'

'If you were ensuring that you got enough to eat,' Beattie observed caustically, 'then that in itself would have kept you fully occupied, so no wonder you didn't realise! They could have paraded a dozen police horses dressed in Christmas tree lights through the room and you wouldn't have noticed a thing.'

'Be that as it may,' Percy insisted over the responding chuckles, 'I've definitely seen that woman before, and not at a party like that one. It's those spectacles — I've seen her wearing them somewhere or other, but my mind won't quite focus on where.'

'No wonder, given that there's a wonderful spread on the table to distract you,' Beattie muttered.

'If you know who's responsible, why can't you simply move in and arrest them?' asked Teddy.

'Because "knowing" is not "proving",' Percy told him. 'And it's a little more complicated than that. We believe that this woman in the photograph arranged the murder of her husband in Bethnal Green three years ago, and that somehow, although we don't know *quite* how exactly, it's all connected.'

'Was that during that horrible time when those houses were being demolished, and our upstairs neighbour in Clerkenwell asked you to find her missing niece?' Esther asked.

'The very same,' Percy confirmed, 'and if you recall, you were the one who realised who she was pretending to be when you brought her back out of the East End and reunited her with her aunt.'

'Typical Percy!' Beattie burst out. 'Not content with causing endless worry for the woman he solemnly vowed to love and obey, he even stoops to dragging family members into his sordid working life.'

'I manage the "love" part of it,' Percy replied in his own defence, 'and as for the "obey" part, the minister must have slipped that in while I was concentrating on putting the ring on the correct finger.'

'Aunt Beattie has a valid point, nevertheless,' Lucy chimed in. 'There was one horrible time when he got me to dress up as a ghost in order to drive a poor man under an approaching train. It wasn't until afterwards that he admitted that the veil I was wearing had belonged to a dead woman!'

'The "poor man" to whom you refer pushed his sister off a moving train,' Percy reminded her with a hint of righteous indignation, 'and he drove *himself* under another train when he tried to escape my clutches.'

'In that same case, Percy got me to act as bookkeeper for the same man — a disgusting creep with wandering hands and a sickening obsession with his dead sister,' said Esther. 'If the girl who worked for him hadn't intervened, he'd have strangled me to death! And let's not forget how, more recently, he obliged me to listen to a school matron confessing to the sexual exploitation of boys under her care.'

'In all of those cases that you cite, the Enright women played major roles in bringing dangerous criminals to justice,' Percy insisted, 'and even your Aunt Beattie did her bit when called upon.'

'Only to the extent of posing as a barren woman — which, of course, I am — seeking to adopt a child,' Beattie explained. 'There were no sexual deviants, no dead bodies, and no moving trains involved, thank the merciful Lord.'

'Have you no evidence at all to justify the arrest of the people who run the catering company?' Teddy persisted.

Jack was happy to reply, since he'd be passing on new information to Percy, thereby maintaining the pretence that they were still both working together at New Scotland Yard. 'We've compared the tender submitted by Strand Enterprises, as the catering company are known, with those from other catering firms that submitted a tender,' he said. 'The one from Strand Enterprises was suspiciously low, the implication being that they were determined to get the job.'

'But that's standard commercial practice,' Lucy insisted. 'I'm responsible for all the tenders that Teddy sends out when he's bidding for an architectural commission, and I'll no doubt be submitting lots more for his new consortium. You bid low in order to get the business, so what's so suspicious about that?'

'It was incredibly low,' Jack told her. 'Whereas all the others were quoting ten shillings per head, Strand's was only six. I don't know anything about the profit margins in the catering industry, but it suggests to me that they were almost bidding at cost price in their anxiety to get the contract, knowing that Uncle Percy would be there.'

'For all you know, they make a habit of bidding low,' Lucy argued. 'Do you have any other examples of contracts that they've bid on recently?'

'No,' Percy admitted, seizing the opening, 'but would you like to get one for us?'

It fell silent for a moment before Lucy asked, 'What do you have in mind? Do I have to pretend to be a ghost again?'

'Of course not,' Percy assured her. 'But you're about to have a celebration party for the merging of Teddy's firm with another, are you not?'

'Not necessarily,' Teddy butted in. 'It would all depend on the likely cost.'

'Precisely,' Percy said. 'And in order to determine that, you'll need to get some quotes, won't you?'

'Have a care, Lucy,' Esther murmured. 'Uncle Percy's plotting something, and before you know what you've let yourself in for, you'll be offering yourself as a human sacrifice to some deranged lunatic in a darkened back room.'

'Nonsense!' Percy insisted. 'I'm just suggesting that Lucy obtains some quotes for external catering for, say, sixty guests, at a prestige event at which the sandwiches, pastries and cakes will be of the highest quality, and that she include Strand Enterprises among those invited to tender for the job. If their quote is consistent with the others, then we'll know that the one they submitted for my farewell do was deliberately low to guarantee that they got the opportunity to poison me.'

'According to you,' Beattie muttered, 'I've been trying to do that to you for years with my cooking.'

There were more chuckles, then Jack rejoined the conversation. 'It may be our only way forward in this case,' he told his sister, 'and you would be the obvious person to achieve it.'

'Why can't you send someone else, like a plain clothes police officer?' Esther demanded.

Percy shook his head. 'These people are not stupid, Esther. They'd spot a subterfuge a mile away, and we need someone with a genuine case — and a woman, what's more, since men don't normally organise parties. And don't think that they won't make surreptitious enquiries into whether or not there is indeed about to be a merger between two local businesses.'

'So you suspect them of being on guard against investigations into their activities?' Teddy asked.

'Wouldn't *you* be?' Percy countered. 'If someone comes to you with a request for architectural services for a proposed development, you surely make discreet enquiries as to whether or not it's a genuine prospect, and — perhaps more to the point — whether or not they'd be likely to have the wherewithal to pay you?'

'Yes, of course,' Teddy conceded. 'So you want Lucy to approach these people for a quote for a celebration party?'

'Among others, yes,' Percy confirmed. 'To make it look genuine, she'll need to approach a few other caterers as well, because Strand will almost certainly make enquiries regarding who else she's been to see. But of course, given Esther's far from glowing testimonials regarding the potential dangers of working undercover, you'd be forgiven for refusing to allow Lucy to undertake even such a safe and simple task.'

'I don't need Teddy's permission to do anything!' Lucy protested loudly. 'I'm an independent woman living in a society in which women are at long last free to follow their own ambitions without the need to seek their husbands' permission for anything! A nation headed by a *queen*, let me remind you! Take Esther — she's about to launch an independent career as a teacher, and I'd wager any amount of money that she didn't need Jack's permission.'

'So you'll do it?' Percy asked triumphantly, since his ruse appeared to have met with success.

Esther gave a groan. 'Hook, line and sinker! He got me to take impossible risks by employing a similar tactic, Lucy. No doubt when you call in at this catering firm's office, you'll find yourself confronted by an axe-wielding maniac hiding behind a door!'

'I haven't agreed to do it yet,' Lucy insisted. 'For one thing, I don't have the time. Tomorrow we'll be travelling back into town with the children, on Tuesday we have the final dress rehearsal for *The Taming of the Shrew* at the theatre, and — well, I have lots of paperwork to prepare for the merger.'

'So Wednesday would be convenient?' Percy asked quietly. 'Or would that not suit Teddy?'

'I already told you,' Lucy responded hotly, 'I don't need his permission to do anything!'

'So Wednesday morning, or Wednesday afternoon?' Percy persisted.

Beattie shook her head and announced, 'No more lamb for you, Judas.'

Lucy looked embarrassed by the ferocity of her protests, and nodded. 'Just to prove my independence, we'll make it Wednesday morning. I'll call in at a few other catering concerns with the same request, then make this Strand outfit my fourth or fifth. How will I let you know the outcome? Will I call into your office at Scotland Yard?'

'What if I were to make a home visit to your delightful residence in Holborn for afternoon tea on Wednesday?' Percy suggested, and Lucy agreed.

'You just fell for Percy's ongoing obsession with his stomach,' said Beattie with a sigh.

'Let's change the subject, shall we?' Esther suggested. 'Lily's been asked to organise the costumes for the Christmas play at school, no doubt because of the proven dressmaking skills of her mother.'

CHAPTER TWELVE

'You really don't have to see me off,' Esther insisted as she and Jack walked together up Church Lane, hand in hand, with Bertie and Lily racing ahead of them.

'You're more in need of my support today than you were even on your first visit to Church Lane, to meet my mother,' Jack insisted.

Esther gripped his hand in a silent gesture of appreciation. 'I had no idea of where we were, and why,' she said, chuckling. 'You left it until the last minute to announce that we'd reached your childhood home, and I just thought we were on a walk in the country. That seems so long ago now.'

'And no regrets, I hope?' Jack asked.

Esther stopped, turned, then stretched upwards in order to give him a warm kiss. 'Until that day, I was Esther Jacobs, a poor Jewish girl living in a horrible single room overlooking a cat food yard in a slum tenement, taking in sewing for a living. Now I'm a comfortably off housewife, married to the most attentive man in the world, and with four adorable children. So what do *you* think? And yesterday, when Lucy was insisting that she didn't need Teddy's permission for anything, she was able to cite *me* as a prime example of a free woman inside a happy marriage. *Thank you*, Jack Enright.'

'And today you take your first step towards realising your dream to become a teacher,' said Jack. 'Are you nervous?'

'Yes. Until now I've been able to lie to myself that I don't know if I'm any good as a teacher because I've never had the opportunity to test myself in formal training. Now I'm about to find out.'

'Whatever happens, you should know that I believe you can do anything you set your mind to,' Jack assured her. 'You survived all those horrible years as an orphan in Spitalfields, which is hardly the ideal place for a woman to be living alone, and you've risen to every challenge that you've been set. Sewing, bookwork, child-rearing — even the occasional criminal investigation. But, putting all that to one side, you're still the most beautiful woman I've ever met, and I can't believe that you chose me.'

'Stop it! You'll have me crying, and I'll arrive for my first day as a teacher in training with a blotchy face,' Esther protested. 'Here's the school coming up, so let go of my hand. I'm not a child being taken to the gates by a parent.'

'No, you're a proud lady taking her children to the school gates, attended by their father and the man who loves you,' said Jack. 'If the other women get jealous, that's their problem.'

'There won't be many other women,' Esther replied. 'Look for yourself — most children have to find their own way to Barking Board School, and some days I worry myself sick that they'll be hit by a wagon or a horse bus, or perhaps be kidnapped by evil men.'

'Aren't there also evil women?' Jack challenged her.

'There are,' Esther confirmed. 'If you only knew what some of these children have to put up with at home. There's no charge for children attending here, but even so I hear stories from some of the children that their brothers and sisters have been held back from getting an education because their parents need them to work on farms, or in warehouses. That's part of the reason why I've chosen teaching, I think — to give the best possible start to the fortunate ones. Anyway, give Bertie and Lily a kiss, and we'll just walk on. Normally I go inside with them, but today they'll be going in without me.'

At the horse bus stop they talked for a few minutes more, then as the service to Poplar via East Ham clattered towards them, Jack gave Esther a final kiss and warm wishes. He then held back so as not to embarrass her as she stepped up into the vehicle and walked down its length until a large lady with a bag full of vegetables shifted to one side, and Esther was able to squeeze between her and a labourer.

Ten swaying minutes later, she made her way off the bus and into the road, looked up at the building that would be her 'school' for the next month, and walked smartly up its short flight of steps and through its main doors with five minutes to spare before class.

Emily Allsop gave a welcome speech to the fifteen new teacher trainees. 'Today you will be getting to know each other and those who will be guiding your studies,' she announced.

For the next twenty minutes, each of the new trainees was asked to rise from their seat and introduce themselves. Most were like Esther — middle-class housewives whose children were now capable of looking after themselves, or who had family servants who could look after them — but almost none of them seemed to have had as much practical experience as Esther.

As for those who would guide their studies, there were only two teachers, and two streams of study. Emily explained that she would take the morning classes from nine until eleven, which would consist of what she called 'technique and application'. From one o'clock until three, the students would undertake 'curriculum' studies with a pale-looking young man called Simon Pendlebury, who had an interesting history. He was Oxford-educated in what they called the 'Classics', and had been a housemaster and games instructor at one of the nation's more prestigious public schools, until he'd undertaken volunteer army training and suffered a horrendous accident that had necessitated the amputation of his left leg. His compensation from a 'regretful' government had been the job that he was now engaged in. He leaned on his cane to support his false leg as he tactfully explained that he would be plugging the gaps in the trainees' grasp of basic subjects, most notably reading, writing and arithmetic.

If Esther were to be honest with herself, she found the afternoon sessions boring, and she suspected that she already knew more about reading and writing than Mr Pendlebury did — and probably a good deal more about basic arithmetic, given her previous experience of bookkeeping, first for a Jewish tailor who'd been an old family friend, and then for an emerging women's trade union that had ceased to exist when its founder had been murdered. She found the 'technique and application' class much more stimulating.

Because Esther had considerable experience in teaching classes of local children, she was able to assess what Miss Allsop was advocating as 'recommended teaching practice' in the harsh light of reality. She was therefore able to offer robust views on what should go on in a classroom, which seemed to impress Emily, as well as being of great interest to the rest of the class.

While Esther had been eagerly experiencing the first day of her new life as a student of education practice, Percy Enright had been partly concealed in the doorway of a bootmaker's shop on Darnley Road, across from Kendrick's Bakery. He was watching the premises intently as he lit up his second pipe of the day and hoped that the bootmaker inside wouldn't insist that he move on. Shortly after ten o'clock, he was rewarded by the sight of a closed wagon rolling into place outside the bakery, with 'Bluntstone Carriers' painted proudly down its side. Down from the running board stepped a familiar figure from his distant past, while from the baker's shop came the youth Percy had encountered on his previous visit, carrying various trays from the shop to the wagon over the course of the next ten minutes. Business was obviously brisk for both tradesmen.

After a leisurely mutton pie and pint in the Fox and Hounds two doors down from the local police station, Percy strolled along Mare Street, then turned right into London Lane until he reached the yard alongside the railway sidings from which Albert Bluntstone conducted his carriage business. There was a faint tinkle from the rusty bell above the front door as Percy pushed his way in and asked to speak to the proprietor. From a back office emerged old Albert Bluntstone, his face a testament to the number of drunken brawls in which he'd come second. He'd only been locked up for his own safety, such had been Percy's charity in 'the good old days'.

'I'm sober today, you old bugger,' Albert said.

Percy nodded. 'You need to be, driving that wagon all over the place, but it's good to see that you've still got customers, despite your fondness for Marston's Best Bitter. And I had occasion to note that one of your customers is Kendrick's Bakery.'

'Wanna mug o' Rosie?' Albert asked.

Percy accepted the invitation, moving into Albert's 'office', which more closely resembled an explosion in a paper warehouse.

'Yer still a rozzer?' Albert demanded. 'We ain't seen you around 'ere for years. An' if yer enquirin' about Kendrick's, then yer must still be.'

'One should never leap to conclusions,' Percy hedged, unwilling to risk prosecution for masquerading as a police officer. 'But tell me about Kendrick's anyway, and why you think I might be interested in it. Do they give you a lot of business?'

'One o' me best customers,' Albert said, 'so I 'ope yer not about to nick 'im for somethin'. Mind you, 'e's a bit snooty sometimes — not like the old man 'e bought the place from, what were a regular drinkin' pal o' mine.'

'Yes, *too* regular for the pair of you, as I recall,' Percy said. 'But the new man — does he send you far with that wagon of yours?'

'Inter London pretty regular,' Albert replied. 'But always the same place.'

'Essex Street, just off the Strand in Covent Garden?'

'More like the Temple than Covent Garden — but just off the Strand, right enough,' Albert confirmed. 'But 'ow did yer know that?'

'Once a rozzer, always a rozzer,' Percy said as he tapped his nose. 'And this doesn't get any blunter with the passing years.'

'I 'opes yer won't be ruinin' me best contract,' Albert replied.

Percy chuckled. 'Maybe giving you a less snooty proprietor to deal with in future, but that's all. Thanks for the drink. I'll leave you to clean up after that strong gale that obviously came through here.'

Percy retraced his steps up to Darnley Road in time to see William Henderson supervising the cleaning of the counter displays inside Kendrick's at the end of a day's business. He looked up as Percy entered, then scuttled back into his office. Percy made his way round the back of the counter, pushed his way past the apprentice, and followed Henderson into his office, closing the door behind him as he confronted his quarry.

'Who are you and what are you doing in my office?' Henderson demanded in that blustering manner with which Percy was all too familiar.

'I'm here about the little matter of how you come to be the proprietor of this bakery,' Percy told him. 'You're not a descendent of old Kendrick, are you? You bought the place off the previous proprietor, who was an old drunk.'

'So? It always pays to tell little lies in business,' Henderson replied. 'If the customers think that it's been in the family for generations, they're more likely to trust the product. So what?'

'So where did the money come from?'

'None of your damned business,' Henderson replied hotly.

'It was a bribe from your police days, wasn't it?' Percy challenged him. 'From a grateful lady to whom you turned a blind eye after she'd just murdered her husband. Along with a man called George Mulherron, who I had the pleasure of shooting dead a few nights ago.'

'What did he tell you, before you shot him?' Henderson asked in a voice quivering with apprehension.

Percy saw his chance. 'That when the widow came to collect the gold watch, you recognised her as the woman who'd been with Mulherron as they fled from the scene of their crime — the murder of Thomas Benton. And that you took a fat bribe to keep your mouth shut, then resigned from the force.'

'I only took what I needed to buy this business,' Henderson admitted with a sigh, losing all vestiges of bravado.

'How much *was* that, exactly?' Percy asked.

'Fifteen hundred pounds. I kept the gold watch, and got nearly forty pounds for it from a dealer in Hatton Garden. And the woman took me to meet another man who gave me a thousand more to keep my mouth shut about Mulherron, who I knew anyway as a standover man working for anyone who'd pay his fee. There was some suggestion that he'd been involved in a string of murders around Bethnal Green at the time, and this man I met was anxious to keep Mulherron's name out of it. I thought it was strange that such an obvious gent would be handing over money to protect pondlife like Mulherron.'

'And he also gave you a contract to supply his catering business with sandwiches and cakes, didn't he?' Percy asked as further inspiration kicked in.

Henderson nodded. 'What's going to happen now?'

'To you? Nothing, provided that we keep this little conversation to ourselves. What's done is done; no-one needs to know who killed Benton, and I have a particular need to know all you can tell me about the man who runs that catering business in Essex Street. Strand Enterprises, isn't it?'

'Yes, that's right, and the man who owns it is a Mr Spencer. He must have some long-standing relationship with Benton's widow — a woman calling herself "Cora" — because she works in his office. At least, she was there one time when I called in with an unpaid invoice.'

'So Benton's widow now works for this Mr Spencer?'

'I believe so. I recognised her as she has lots of curly red hair.'

'You'll be hearing nothing more from me unless you've been telling me more porkies,' said Percy. 'So just relax and keep mixing the dough.'

'Why do you wish to join the police force?' Jack asked for the fourth time the following morning. He was interviewing potential recruits, but his mind was elsewhere, principally on Esther's bubbling enthusiasm when he'd found her at home on his return from work on Monday afternoon. 'I'm going to learn so much!' she'd announced. 'And I can be back here every afternoon in time to welcome you home.'

Jack forced his mind back to the matter in hand.

'My father was a police officer in Uxbridge before he retired and we moved out to Staines, where he manages a smallholding for his younger brother,' the latest interviewee, Charles Elliot, told him. 'I really don't want to sell cabbages and spuds for a living, and I certainly don't want to spend the rest of my life in dreary old Staines, so I thought I might try my hand at being a bobby. My girl thinks it's a very manly thing to do for a living, and when we're married we could find a couple of rooms somewhere wherever I'd be posted.'

It was an honest answer at least, and better than the usual pretentious rubbish like, 'I want to serve the public' or — even worse — 'I want to make the streets safe for decent people'. Both usually indicated that the applicant was simply after a guaranteed income and was handy with his fists.

'You realise that some of the stations to which you might be assigned are in the East End, where there's a lot of poverty and seemingly never-ending crime?' Jack asked.

'Yes, sir, but that's where you need police constables the most, isn't it?' said Charles. 'I don't mind that prospect.'

'And your wife-to-be?'

'She's from Shoreditch originally, so she knows what life's like down there. She's already told me how proud she'd be to have me patrolling the streets, maintaining the peace.'

'Very well, thank you for coming in for interview, and we'll be in touch one way or the other within a week,' Jack told him.

It was shortly after eleven thirty, and the next scheduled interview wasn't until two o'clock, so it was time for Jack to make his way to the chophouse. He and Percy had agreed on a Tuesday lunchtime meeting at Tan Li's before they'd parted company on Sunday.

The smile on Percy's face as he waved Jack into the vacant seat at their normal side table was promising, so Jack took the seat and asked, 'Why the big smirk, and where have you been since Sunday?'

'Back in Hackney, scaring former Constable William Henderson. He conveniently confirmed that Thomas Benton was indeed murdered by the man I shot dead recently — George Mulherron. As I suspected, Benton's widow, a lady called Cora, had a hand in his death. Henderson recognised the lady when she got greedy and tried to reclaim the gold watch, which Henderson kept for himself. But — and here's the interesting bit — it seems that this Cora wasn't the only one anxious to buy Henderson's silence. Someone he described to me as a "gent" also paid him a thousand pounds to keep the lid on Mulherron's identity, and the only plausible reason for that is that Mulherron was part of Mangler Maguire's team, who were killing those who refused to vacate their homes.'

'So the person who wanted you dead might well have been seeking revenge for the death of Maguire, which we originally thought was extremely unlikely,' Jack replied.

'Well, here's something else that's extremely unlikely,' said Percy as a meat pie appeared on the table before him. 'Henderson said that the same lady who became a widow on the death of Thomas Benton is now working for Strand Enterprises. She's in some sort of clerical role, which might explain why she knew nothing about how to manage a retirement party, and couldn't even work out which beer glass to put the poison in.'

'How do we prove that she actually committed the deed?' Jack asked.

Percy shrugged. 'I'll tell you that when I've worked it out. But don't forget to meet me at Lucy's for afternoon tea tomorrow. Now, let me remind you that it's your turn to pay, even though you supplied lunch on Sunday, which doesn't count.'

CHAPTER THIRTEEN

Lucy took a deep breath, then pushed open the door beside the bookshop on Essex Street. She then climbed up the staircase until she reached the glass door that claimed to be the entrance to Strand Enterprises. A bell suspended over the door gave a warning tinkle as she pushed it open, and a smart-looking bespectacled woman of about thirty-five years of age emerged from behind the office counter. She was dressed in a charcoal-grey skirt and jacket, and smiled ingratiatingly at Lucy as she asked, 'Good morning, madam, and what can I do for you today?'

'I'm Mrs Lucy Masefield,' Lucy replied with a nervous catch in her throat that she hoped wasn't too audible, 'and I am looking for a quote for a buffet for some sixty or so people.'

'And how did you learn of Strand Enterprises?' the woman asked in a friendly, matter-of-fact sort of way. Fortunately, Lucy had been primed on that by Uncle Percy, and she replied, 'From my brother, who attended a farewell party for which you supplied the catering. He was particularly complimentary about the manner in which the event was organised and catered for, with particular reference to the excellent cakes.'

'Sixty people, you said?' the woman asked.

'Give or take. I'm hoping that you can supply me with a quote per head, and from that we can estimate how many we can afford to invite.'

'Is it a private party?'

'No — more of a business function, really,' Lucy replied, on more comfortable ground. 'My husband is an architect in practice in Holborn, and he's recently been invited to merge his business with that of a building enterprise that has plans to erect quality houses in various parts of north London that are currently undeveloped. We're anxious for it to be celebrated in style, which is why we're following up on the excellent recommendation from my brother.'

'He attended one of our recently catered functions?'

'He did indeed.'

'And which one was that?'

Lucy froze, uncertain whether or not to make reference to the function at which a senior police officer was murdered, perhaps by someone within this enterprise. 'He didn't say, exactly — only that it was a splendid send-off for some senior man who was retiring. It was somewhere in Westminster, I believe.'

'And what exactly were you seeking by way of refreshments?'

'The usual,' Lucy said as she slowly breathed out a long sigh of relief. 'Sandwiches, pastries such as sausage rolls and pork pies, fancy cakes, and a good supply of beer.'

The woman gave her a long, hard look. 'If you'd care to take a seat, Mrs — um, what was it again?'

'Mrs Masefield — Lucy Masefield.'

'Yes, as I say, if you'd care to take a seat, I'll see what Mr Spencer can do for you. Only we're fully booked for the next few weeks.'

'It doesn't have to be immediately,' Lucy explained, 'since we're still at the planning stage, and the date can be flexible, to accommodate your availability.'

'Very well, I'll see what Mr Spencer says.'

She moved along the back of the counter to a door on which she tapped lightly, then walked in without any apparent indication that she'd been invited to do so. She closed the door behind her once inside, so Lucy was unable to hear any conversation that might be taking place. Then, after what seemed like an eternity, but was probably no more than a few minutes, the door opened again, and the lady walked back out, followed by a very smartly dressed man who looked to be in his early fifties.

'Miss Bligh tells me that you're seeking a quote for what sounds like our standard menu — sandwiches, pastries, sweet cakes and beer. Is that correct?' he asked affably.

'Yes, that's right,' Lucy confirmed.

'And we were recommended by your brother, who attended a similar function for which we catered?'

'Er — yes,' Lucy responded nervously.

Mr Spencer's face lost its smile. 'Did your brother tell you how he came to learn who the caterers at that function had been?'

'No — I didn't think it was important. I've obviously sought a few more quotations from other caterers such as yourselves, and he just said, "Try this lot — Strand Enterprises — because they did a splendid job at a celebration I recently attended."'

'Which celebration was that?' Spencer asked as his eyes narrowed slightly.

Again, Lucy was obliged to fudge her answer. 'He didn't say — is it important?'

'What does your brother do by way of a profession?' was the next question.

Suddenly, Lucy was struck by inspiration. 'He plays the piano in a small quartet that often gets hired for private functions.'

'Do you remember a quartet at any recent function?' Spencer asked Miss Bligh, who shook her head. Spencer seemed relieved to learn that.

'Pardon my inquisitiveness, but there was a recent event at which — well, we needn't go into that. Suffice to say that it had a most unfortunate ending, and I was hoping that you hadn't received an unnecessarily negative view of our services.'

'No — my brother just said that the food was excellent. Mind you, it's not every event that he attends at which the hired musicians get to partake of the food, so perhaps he was overly impressed.'

'I'm sure that wasn't the case, Mrs Masefield. If you'll just wait there a moment, I'll make a few calculations, then supply you with a written quote. Perhaps Miss Bligh could make you a cup of tea while you wait.'

'There's no need, really,' Lucy insisted. 'I have other calls on my time this morning, so if you could just let me have your quote, I won't take up any more of your time.'

She waited nervously as Spencer disappeared into his office, and Miss Bligh appeared to be attending to paperwork on the counter in front of her. Then the inner office door reopened, and Spencer emerged holding a single sheet of paper.

'There you go, Mrs Masefield. I hope you'll find that it's the most attractive offer to suit your needs. Hopefully we'll be hearing from you again shortly.'

After the Wednesday morning class at the teacher training college, as the students were filing out of the classroom on their way to the cafeteria down the main hallway, Emily Allsop said quietly to Esther, 'Have you got a moment, Mrs Enright?'

Esther held back, then when the final student had left the room, Emily said, 'I have something important that I want to talk to you about, and it might be more convenient if we did that in my office, after you've had some lunch. I'll have some tea waiting for you.'

'If it's not too presumptuous of me,' Esther replied, fearful that she was about to be admonished for her forthright opinions in class, and anxious to get it out of the way, 'I only purchase tea in the cafeteria anyway. I bring a sandwich in every day.'

'Excellent!' Emily replied. 'Then you can eat your sandwich while we share a pot of tea.'

In Emily's office, seated in the visitor's chair, Esther fumbled nervously as she opened the bag that contained her modest daily cheese sandwich. Her temples began to throb as she waited for Emily to finish pouring the tea.

'Esther, I wish you to treat what I'm about to tell you with the greatest of confidence, and whatever the outcome of our resulting discussions, I wish it to go no further. Do I have your assurance on that?'

'Of course,' Esther murmured, leaving her sandwich where it was, but taking a nervous sip of tea in order to moisten her drying throat.

'Well, the truth is that I shall be leaving here when the current course ends,' Emily confided. 'I was, as you may have guessed, for some years a teacher myself, in a *very* fashionable ladies' college in Eastbourne, which is on the south coast. It was much favoured by ladies in somewhat reduced, but nevertheless genteel, circles during what they are fond of calling their "season". Then for reasons that we need not go into, but which concerned a matter of the heart, I found it appropriate to resign from that post and apply for the one that I currently hold. But I miss standing in front of a class and seeing their eager faces — an experience that you clearly relish, given what you've already shared with us in class — and now the opportunity to do so again has arisen. Do please eat your sandwich, Esther.'

Esther took her first bite, relieved that Miss Allsop didn't seem to want to reprimand her.

'It's a small private school almost in the centre of Watford. Are you familiar with Watford at all?'

Esther shook her head.

'It's a delightful country town in Hertfordshire, only twenty miles north of London, and increasingly popular with those who can take advantage of the excellent train service from there into town. In the main they're professional and commercial people, and they have burgeoning families and the wherewithal to afford a decent education for their children. Anyway, this opens up the market for private schools, for which the parents pay fees in order for their progeny to attend. Not like the Board Schools with which you are already familiar, but more like institutions in which the pupils can learn to make their way in comfortable society with the benefit of a rounded education, and not just reading, writing and arithmetic. One of these schools has now become available.'

'For purchase, you mean?' Esther asked.

'Yes. The previous headmistress resigned about a year ago, and the school's been going steadily downhill ever since, with the pupil roll less than half what it was during its halcyon days. The original proprietor has been dead for some years, with only two spinster sisters left to run the business, and now they wish to sell up and move to Eastbourne. That's how I learned about the school, from a former colleague there who was approached in case she might be interested in purchasing the entire business, along with the family home across the road. The headmistress is provided with accommodation inside the school, and I now have the opportunity to become the new headmistress and purchase the entire enterprise.'

'It sounds very exciting,' Esther observed as she sipped her tea and started on her second sandwich. 'I'm only glad that you won't be leaving until after I've finished this course. These things can't be achieved in three weeks, can they? If I'm fortunate, I'll be accredited by the time you leave.'

It fell silent for a moment, then Emily looked Esther in the eye and asked, 'How would you like to become accredited at the end of *this* week?'

Esther put down the remains of her second sandwich, too shocked to reply immediately, and Emily took advantage of her silence.

'There's nothing we can teach you here that you don't already know, Esther. You are the finest, most natural teacher I've ever had on any of my courses, and since the matter of accreditation is left entirely to me, I could sign off on you with no qualms of conscience. Then I'd like you to come and work with me at my new school.'

'Forgive me for asking,' Esther replied hesitantly, 'but will you still give me accreditation if I just go back to Barking Board School?'

'Of *course*,' Emily told her, 'and I'm sorry if that came across as some sort of bribe. I can assure you that the two matters are unrelated. You can have your accreditation on Friday, whatever you intend to do with it. But — independently of that — I'd be delighted if you'd join me at Cassiobury House as my second teacher, deputy headmistress, in effect.'

Esther was speechless. What she was being offered was the equivalent of a street vendor being given the management of a West End department store, and she felt as if she were dreaming. Eventually, she managed a few words of acknowledgement. 'It's a most generous offer, but there are so many things I have to consider before I can accept, as I'd *dearly* love to. The school is in Watford, you say? Do you know if I could get a horse bus there from Barking every day, or perhaps a train?'

Emily shook her head. 'There's a house in its own grounds, at the entrance to the Cassiobury Estate, and across the road from the school. The proprietors who are selling the school are prepared to sell that house for a thousand pounds to whoever takes the business off their hands. If I buy the school, you could buy the house.'

'I have a husband and four children to think about,' Esther reminded her.

'It has four bedrooms and a cottage of sorts in a garden to the rear, for the use of domestic staff.'

'But my husband has to travel into London every day for his work,' said Esther.

This time, Emily frowned. 'As I already mentioned, there is an excellent train service from Watford to Euston Station in London, and a horse bus that runs from the Cassiobury Estate entrance to the station. And I seem to recall that during your recruitment interview, you assured us that your husband was fully supportive of your ambition to be a teacher.'

'As indeed he is,' Esther confirmed, 'but that was when we thought that I'd be returning to teach in Barking, not Watford.'

'Obviously it would be a great deal to ask of him,' Emily conceded, 'but how strong is your marriage, if that's not an impertinent question?'

'*Very* strong,' Esther asserted as she contemplated what she had to persuade Jack to agree to, and how to approach the issue. 'He'll need a great deal of persuasion, obviously, but I think I know how to get around him.'

'Well, I suggest that you test the water without delay, because by the end of this week you'll be an accredited teacher, *wherever* it is that you're destined to take your talents next.'

'I'm almost certain that he was suspicious,' Lucy told Jack and Percy as she laid the tall metal serving tower down on the table and Percy reached for a ham sandwich. 'I was *very* happy to get out of there, let me tell you. If you want someone else to go back in there, count me out. Anyway, here's your written quote.' She handed Jack the piece of paper she'd been given by Mr Spencer.

Jack took it from her, read it and told Percy, 'It's for ten shillings.'

'What made you think he was suspicious?' Percy asked between mouthfuls.

'It was when he asked how I'd come to learn about Strand Enterprises, and I was caught out for an answer,' said Lucy. 'I tried to lie my way out of that, as you suggested, by saying that my brother had recommended them, and then his face sort of clouded over, and he asked what my brother did for a living. I couldn't tell him he was a police officer, obviously, so I told him that he played the piano in a quartet that had been hired for some function at which they'd been doing the catering. He asked his assistant — a "Miss Bligh" — whether she recalled any such ensemble playing at any recent function, to which she said no.'

'As far as we know,' Jack told her as he reached for a buttered scone, 'if she's who we think she is, she only attended one of those "recent functions", and that was the one at which Montague was poisoned. Was this her, by any chance?' He reached inside his jacket and slid the photograph of "Miss Cora" onto the table between them.

'Yes, that was her,' Lucy confirmed.

'She was once "Mrs Benton". Perhaps "Bligh" was her unmarried name,' said Percy. 'Anyway, she arranged the murder of her husband, who was a former police officer in the

West End, and was even present at it. At least now we can tie her in with the Bethnal Green murders, the goings-on at Strand Enterprises, and the poisoning that may well have been intended for me. She's clearly a lady of many faces, and I wish I could remember where I've seen her before. It's really bothering me, given my memory for faces.'

'She seemed quite at ease in a secretarial role, anyway,' Lucy told them both as she poured the tea. 'I got the feeling that she and Mr Spencer were close, if you get my meaning.'

'They're clearly collaborators in the matter of murder, anyway,' Percy observed as he reached for his second slice of seedcake.

'All the more reason why I've no intention of going back there,' Lucy insisted. 'Try Esther next time.'

'There probably won't be any further need to send someone in there,' Jack suggested, 'and Esther's done her bit for the Met over the years. It would be more than our marriage is worth to ask her to do so again.'

'Let's hope you're right,' Percy muttered. 'Anyway, thank you, Lucy — for doing that, and for this delightful afternoon tea.'

'Have you bought a new outfit, or something?' Jack asked Esther that evening as Alice placed his favourite lamb chops in front of them both and assured them that the children had eaten all their sausages in the kitchen.

'No, why do you ask?' Esther asked disingenuously.

'Well, I only normally get lamb chops when you need to tell me about something you've done, or bought, or perhaps when you want something and are trying to butter me up.'

'It might also be because we're celebrating,' Esther suggested.

'Celebrating what, exactly?' he asked.

Esther paused dramatically before replying, 'I'll be an accredited teacher by the end of this week.'

'I thought the course you're on took a month.'

'It does — normally. But Miss Allsop called me into her room today and told me that she's happy to accredit me on Friday.'

'You must have really impressed her — well done!'

Esther waited until he was into his second chop, then said, 'Miss Allsop also offered me a teaching position.'

'What, at that college in East Ham?'

'No, at a select private school in Watford.'

'That's miles away, across country. Could you travel there every day?'

'Not as far as I know, but there's a house available just across the road from the school.'

Jack looked carefully at her face for a moment, then asked, 'Does that explain the lamb chops? You want us all to move to Watford? Or were you thinking of leaving me to bring up the children?'

'Obviously not, but there's apparently a good rail service from Watford into London, so you'd hardly notice the difference. And Miss Allsop was most impressed by the fact that I'm one of the few women whose careers aren't held back by their husbands.'

'But it wouldn't be just your husband holding you back, would it?' Jack pointed out. 'There's the children to think about, and this is the house where I was born and raised, the house I hope to leave to our children.'

'So you don't approve of the idea, even though it would be the most amazing, most prestigious, most...'

'That's *precisely* how I feel, lamb chops or no lamb chops,' Jack replied in a tone of finality.

Esther let the matter drop. She'd just have to wait until Jack wanted something important from her, and she could only hope that the opportunity presented itself before Emily Allsop changed her mind.

CHAPTER FOURTEEN

'Stand right there, Percy Enright, where I can get a good look at you and see more lies written across your deceitful face!' Beattie bellowed at her husband before he'd even hung his coat up.

Since he was uncertain which of the many lies he'd told her in recent weeks she was referring to, Percy opted for silence, knowing from bitter experience that Beattie would soon fill it.

'Where have you been, and what have you been doing, for the past three weeks?' she demanded.

Percy, the master of half-truths, had a ready answer for that. 'Investigating why someone poisoned Chief Superintendent Montague in a failed attempt to poison me. Why do you ask?'

'I'll tell you why I asked, Percy Enright! I called into Scotland Yard today.'

'And why was that?' Percy asked, hoping to buy himself some valuable time to invent a plausible alibi.

'I'd been shopping in Piccadilly, and already had an armful of heavy parcels before I'd finished, so I thought it would be a good idea to call into the Yard and ask that you keep them in your office for the day, then bring them home this evening. I was told by a *very* helpful sergeant at the front desk that you weren't in.'

'As I said, I was out investigating. Lucy very obligingly made that enquiry for us, and Jack and I then joined her for afternoon tea.'

'It's to be hoped that you ate sufficient to last you until breakfast, because there'll be no more poisoning attempts against you in *this* house this evening, after what I *also* learned.'

'Which was?' Percy asked, in the hope that he could still brazen it out.

'You are no longer on the force — you retired last week. Imagine my embarrassment, as the wife who didn't even know that her husband had retired!'

'As I already explained,' Percy tried in a last-ditch attempt to avoid the deluge, 'my retirement was postponed while I handled this latest enquiry.'

'I tried suggesting that to the man on the front desk, and he sent for a *very* senior officer — a man called Bruce — who explained to me, in a tone of voice that he's no doubt employed over the years to explain to widows how their husbands had died, that your extended retirement had been cancelled after you shot a man dead in Bethnal Green. When were you going to share that little titbit with me?'

'What, that I'd shot a man who was coming for me with a heavy hammer, or the fact that I'm now officially retired?'

'Don't fence with me, Percy Enright! And don't try any of your treacle words to explain it all away, because I took the further step of calling in at our bank. Mr Enderby was able to advise me that last Thursday our account received the first of what will apparently be an ongoing series of payments from a source described as the "Metropolitan Police Retirement Fund".'

'That's reassuring, anyway,' Percy muttered, but it didn't mollify his wife.

'Why have you been leaving here every day, as if you were still employed as a police officer, and coming home looking drained and frustrated as usual?' she demanded. 'What have you *really* been up to?'

'Like I said, trying to find out why someone wanted me dead.'

'At this precise moment, you need look no further than your own front hall!' Beattie thundered. 'Are you seriously expecting me to swallow that you're still involved in a police investigation when you're no longer a police officer?'

'It's a personal matter,' Percy replied as he felt the resentment building up inside him. 'I don't see why I should have to stand here like a naughty schoolboy and explain why I want to find out who murdered Herbert Montague.'

'Then perhaps you shouldn't *behave* like a naughty schoolboy! Did you really think I'd object to you continuing with your enquiries?'

'If you don't, then why are we having this conversation?'

'Because I'm not satisfied with your answer. The Met employs hundreds of men — some of them more able and experienced than you — who can carry out the investigations you claim to be conducting. I rather think that you've been up to something else.'

'Like what?'

'Another woman?' she asked as her voice cracked slightly, giving him hope that the storm had now resolved itself into a summer breeze.

He stepped forward and pulled her to him. 'One woman has always been enough for me, Beattie Enright. I could no more be unfaithful to you than I could go on a diet.'

'Well, that's something, I suppose,' she muttered over his right shoulder. 'But you're such a skilful liar that I never know what's the truth and what isn't with you.'

'If you want to be reassured that I've been telling you the truth, then ask Jack.'

Beattie snorted. 'You've got your nephew well trained enough to lie through a six-inch-thick plank of wood for you, so that's no reassurance.'

'Then try Lucy.'

'Your niece? You got her involved in these underhand enquiries while we were at Sunday lunch, didn't you?'

'We call them "undercover" enquiries, but yes — we did. Esther's made it very plain that she no longer wants to become involved in our little exploits, and now Lucy's insisting the same.'

'And how much longer do you think this latest "little exploit" will last?' Beattie demanded. 'Even if I accept your confession, I need to know when Percy Enright will strike his last blow for justice and start wallpapering Jack's old room.'

The following day, at their lunchtime meeting at Tan Li's, Percy told Jack what had transpired with Beattie.

'You'll have to back me up that I've been continuing to investigate Strand Enterprises,' he said gloomily.

'Do you think she'll believe me?' Jack asked.

'No, judging by one of the many accusations she levelled at me. It was like being in one of my own cells, being interrogated by a very determined and experienced rozzer of the old school.'

'So you're off the case?' Jack asked in dismay.

Percy smiled for the first time that day. 'No, as it happens. She was so delighted by my assurance that I'd not been with another woman that she gave me permission to continue until we nail whoever tried to feed me a cyanide shandy.'

'All we need to do now is decide how to prove that it came from Strand Enterprises, by the hand of "Miss Cora" or "Miss Bligh", whichever hat she's wearing when we buckle her,' Jack replied. 'Anyway, speaking of wives, Esther's going to get her teacher accreditation in less than half the time it normally takes. She's very pleased, of course, and now she's got some wild idea about moving to Watford to teach at some school there.'

'Leaving you in Barking?'

'No, she wants to take us all with her. Imagine that.'

'I can't. What did you tell her?'

'I said it was out of the question. She seemed to accept that, although she was particularly loving at bedtime, so I think she might circle round for another try before much longer.'

'Be strong, my boy. There'll come a time when the only attraction of bedtime is a good night's sleep. Now, back to Strand Enterprises, once we've placed our orders.'

Once they had ordered their food, Jack said, 'It's even clearer that Strand underbid in order to get the contract for your farewell do. They quoted Lucy ten shillings a head for precisely the same thing that they only wanted six for when they were intent on poisoning you. Have we got enough to nick them on suspicion?'

'Suspicion of what? Sharp business practice?' Percy asked as he attacked his second chop. 'No, but from what Lucy said, it seems that Mr Spencer was a bit rattled by the reference to previous events that they'd catered for. Perhaps if we were to shake their bars a bit more robustly, they might give something away.'

'Lucy swore she wasn't prepared to go back there.'

'Which is a pity, because if we could confront them with the ten shillings that they're quoting for the same thing that they only charged six for at "a certain recent function", that might loosen someone's tongue. The trouble is that they know me by sight, and might even take the opportunity to kill me by other means if I show my face in there. Miss Bligh isn't above murder, remember.'

154

'I suppose I could go in there pretending to be Teddy, and demanding to know why their quote's so high,' Jack suggested.

Percy shook his head. 'You were at my retirement do as well, and were seen talking to me. And we can't ask Teddy, because he's the man whose party it's supposed to be. He'd hardly be taking personal management of something as minor as an office bunfight. That sort of thing is left to bookkeepers.'

Their eyes met across the lunch table, and Jack shook his head vigorously.

'If you're thinking what I *think* you're thinking, forget it. Esther said never again, remember?'

'She's said that *several* times in the past, as I recall,' Percy reminded him, 'yet she nevertheless went in to bat for us afterwards.'

'She said she meant it after last time, with that crooked school matron.'

'But this time there's a little matter of a teaching job in — where was it, Watford?'

'Yes, Watford,' Jack said with a grimace.

'Watford's not so bad,' Percy assured him. 'At least it's got a football team, and the trains go there all the time from Euston.'

'So Esther told me,' Jack replied, 'but the answer's still no.'

'Not even if it will finally give us the evidence against whoever tried to poison your dear old uncle, the man who brought you up, encouraged you to join the police force, covered for you with your aunt when you broke the living room window with a cricket ball...'

'It's still no,' Jack said firmly.

'And the man who won't tell Esther that you were ogling that red-haired waitress at my party?'

'You wouldn't.'

'I might.'

'You're a conniving, unprincipled, sneaky…'

'Flattery won't deter me.'

'The red-haired waitress is just the woman we're seeking, remember?'

'I might tell Esther that, in the hope that she misunderstands. Something along the lines of, "Jack was just telling me the other day that he's seeking this woman he met at a party, who has striking red hair and…"'

'You're a scoundrel, do you know that?' Jack sighed. 'I'll try to talk Esther into it, but not necessarily with any reference to Watford.'

'It always gives me a deep sense of satisfaction when you see things my way. Now, let's settle up and go our separate ways, shall we? I promised Beattie I'd look at wallpaper in our local hardware store. After all, there's no harm in looking, and if I can't quite find what I have in mind, well, I'll just have to live with the disappointment, won't I?'

'Tell me more about this offer in Watford,' Jack said to Esther as she sighed for the fifth time since supper while poring over one of the practice manuals she'd bought from the teacher training college.

She looked up for long enough to show that she was far from prepared to engage in warm conversation, then looked down again at what she'd been reading.

'I might be interested to learn more,' Jack offered, and this time she held his gaze.

'What's changed since we mentioned it briefly over supper, and you once again rejected the idea?' she asked tersely, and he assessed that the time was right.

'Well, my reason for rejecting the whole idea was the fact that I'm so deeply involved in the investigation into who tried to poison Uncle Percy. It's not just any old investigation, because Percy's my uncle. I owe him so much, and —'

'At least you never learned to lie as convincingly as him, Jack Enright,' Esther said, cutting in. 'What do I have to do?'

'Beg pardon?'

'Don't even *try* to come the old soldier with me! I'm your wife, and your face is very familiar to me, particularly when it's trying to conceal something. Like that time you tried to give me a surprise birthday party, but couldn't stop yourself from smiling when the first guests started arriving with bottles of wine, and you tried to pretend that it was just a coincidence.'

'What makes you think I'm up to something this time?'

'You first of all make reference to something you wouldn't even let me mention an hour ago, and then you mention work. I can join the dots, Jack. There's something you want me to do in connection with that attempt to poison Percy, and in exchange you'd be prepared to at least consider a move to Watford. Hence my question — what do I have to do?'

'Go to the business premises of the catering company that tried to poison Percy, and enquire why the quote they gave Lucy for her upcoming buffet is so much higher than the quote they supplied to the Met for Percy's send-off party.'

'Thereby revealing that I know that they were behind the poisoning?'

'Not necessarily. You just play the role of the curious bookkeeper employed by Teddy. And you'll only be making that enquiry of the lady behind the counter who's the receptionist.'

'So who can I expect to find lurking behind a door with an axe, or a loaded revolver?'

'We'll make sure that the person we're really after is out at the time. We just want to fire a shot across their bows, and hopefully provoke them into doing something rash.'

'Like silencing me, you mean?'

'Of course not — would I expose you to that sort of danger?'

'You've been known to, and more than once.'

'Well, not this time, I promise. Just a simple enquiry of the woman on the front counter, then out you come.'

'I bask in your reassurance,' Esther said with heavy sarcasm. 'And if I make this "simple enquiry", you'll do what, precisely, in exchange?'

'I'll consider the move to Watford.'

'And if I really *am* exposed to danger?'

'We'll move to Watford.'

'Can I get that in writing?'

'Do you really need that? Can't you trust your own husband?'

'My husband, yes. But I'm not so sure about his uncle.'

CHAPTER FIFTEEN

The following Saturday morning saw them all gathered on a long bench in the churchyard of St Clement Danes, overlooking the Strand, and only yards from the entrance to Essex Street. Clouds of acrid smoke were billowing from Percy's pipe, while Constable Jauncey from Bow Street Police Station was smoking a cigar that he'd purchased a few minutes earlier from a local tobacco shop. Esther was sitting as far away as she could from the smoke, while Jack was seated next to her, hoping that his repeated assurances that she would not be exposed to any danger would be justified. Esther, for her part, was half hoping that there *would* be an element of danger, so that the move to Watford would be beyond Jack's ability to refuse.

The previous day she'd become an accredited teacher. After thanking Emily Allsop profusely for her generosity and assistance, and presenting her with a hand-embroidered kerchief that Lily had completed only the evening before, she'd assured her, 'By hook or by crook, I'll be joining you in Watford.' She smiled to herself at the memory, and the realisation that later that day she'd need to confront a 'crook' in order to achieve her ambition.

'Are you sure they'll be open on a Saturday?' she'd asked when they'd first gathered in the churchyard.

'I sent Constable Venables in there before you and Jack arrived, just to make sure,' Percy had told her. 'He pretended to be following up a complaint about Strand Enterprises wagons blocking Essex Street while loading for their contract catering. Venables confirmed that there was a man in the office, who we believe to be Mr Spencer, and a woman matching the description of the one you'll be confronting behind the counter. He'll let us know if and when the man leaves the premises, so that it'll be safe for you to go in and deal with the woman.'

'And if he *doesn't* leave, then what?' she'd asked.

'Then we try again on Monday. Jack tells me that you've finished your training course, and that you got through it in less than half the time. Well done, and presumably you'll now be free on Monday?'

'If you're prepared to supervise the housework that's been sadly neglected while Alice has been acting as a substitute mother for my four children, then of course.'

There had been no further conversation until Constable Venables rejoined them in the churchyard. 'The pompous geezer that I spoke to earlier just headed off down Essex Street towards the far end, sir,' he said.

'Excellent!' Percy replied, then turned to Esther. 'You know what to do?'

'I ought to,' Esther said starchily, 'since you've reminded me several times in the last hour.'

'And you've got the estimate that Lucy obtained from Strand Enterprises?'

'Of course. Jack passed it to me before we even left the house, and it's in my handbag.'

'Very well, off you go,' Percy instructed her.

Esther turned to give Jack a farewell kiss. 'I'm only doing this in return for the opportunity to follow my dream of becoming a senior teacher in a proper school, so don't even *think* of reneging on your promise to consider it. And if you have to come and rescue me, it's beyond discussion, agreed?'

'Yes, but let's hope that we don't need to,' Jack replied as a shiver ran up his spine. Catching criminals was one thing, but placing his wife in potential danger was something he'd never quite got used to. Not for the first time, he wished that his uncle had become an accountant or a vicar, or anything other than a persuasive police officer with a penchant for deviousness.

Esther strode purposefully out into the Strand, then took the first right into Essex Street, looking for the bookshop down on the right. The sign on the wall displayed an arrow pointing into the alleyway to the side, and after offering a silent prayer she pushed open the door, climbed the stairs and entered the office of Strand Enterprises. A woman of approximately her own age looked up from behind the counter at the sound of the bell ringing above the door, fixed her with a painted smile and asked, 'Yes, madam, what can I do for you this morning?'

'You can explain why you're attempting to charge us more than you recently charged another organisation for precisely the same catering service,' Esther replied in what she hoped sounded like a tone of outrage.

'I beg your pardon?'

'Sorry, let me start again,' Esther replied. 'My name is Esther Jacobs, and I'm a bookkeeper employed by Edward Masefield, the architect, in his office in Holborn. His wife recently obtained a quote from you for a planned function to celebrate the amalgamation of Mr Masefield's firm with a local builder. It's for ten shillings a head, for a *very* standard menu, and for an estimated sixty guests. I've made enquiries, and it seems that this is considerably higher than previous prices you've charged for precisely the same thing. Mr Masefield has asked me to enquire first of all why your estimate is so high, and secondly whether it might be reduced to, say, six shillings a head, like it was for a previous function that I know all about.'

She became aware that a man had entered the office while she'd been making her enquiry with what she hoped was just the right amount of determination. He was now standing a few feet behind her, no doubt waiting politely in what had become a queue for the attention of the clerk.

'May I see the estimate, please?' Miss Bligh asked.

Esther pulled it from her handbag and laid it on the counter.

'Yes, I remember it now,' Miss Bligh confirmed, 'but what makes you believe that it's higher than those we normally quote, and why have you simply not accepted another one?'

'As to your second question,' Esther blustered, 'your pastries are highly recommended by a previous customer — the same one that you only charged six shillings a head for. But see here — ten shillings, which your proprietor assured us was your best quote.'

'I'm sure there must have been some error in the totalling,' Miss Bligh assured Esther. 'If you'd care to come through to the office, I'll see if I can find Mr Spencer's original calculations.'

She lifted the flap in the counter that allowed access to the rear office, and Esther stepped through it and into the empty office whose door Miss Bligh held open. She was followed closely by the man who'd apparently been queuing for service, who pushed Esther hard in the back, causing her to lose her footing on the loose carpet and fall to the floor. Miss Bligh then pulled Esther's hands behind her back, while the man produced a length of cord from a drawer in his office desk and tied her hands together before pulling her to her feet, then pushing her into the chair behind his desk.

'Now then,' he hissed, 'a few simple questions regarding how you came to know about the function for which we charged only six shillings a head. Keep your answers short and truthful, and as an incentive towards that, my associate Cora here will be standing by to make incisions into that beautiful face of yours if you don't.'

On cue, Miss Bligh lifted the hem of her gown to just above her knee, and extracted a long, thin knife that had been tucked into her garter.

'Cora gets jealous of women who're as pretty as she is, so she won't hesitate to carve into your face if I tell her to,' Spencer continued. 'In fact, sometimes it's necessary for me to order her to stop. So, first question — what do you know about the six-shillings-a-head function, and who sent you to enquire? Sorry, that's two questions, but feel free to answer them both very quickly if you want to avoid scars down your lovely cheeks.'

'She should be back by now,' Jack said nervously to Percy as he paced up and down in front of where his uncle was seated, calmly smoking his pipe.

'Not necessarily,' Percy replied serenely. 'These things take time, and the longer she takes, the more we're going to panic Miss Bligh into giving away something important.'

'I'm not convinced,' Jack replied. 'For a start, will she be able to appreciate the significance of the ten shilling quote? It wasn't her who gave it, remember — it was most probably that boss of hers — Spencer Mallory.'

'Who?' Percy demanded, as he knocked the ash from his pipe and leapt to his feet. 'Where did you get that name from?'

'It was on that quote that Lucy got from Mr Spencer. He signed it "Spencer Mallory". I meant to mention it, because the name's vaguely familiar. Did I get round to it?'

'No, you didn't!' Percy snapped as he commanded Constables Jauncey and Venables to come with him and raced off in the direction of Essex Street, adding, 'Leave that halfwit behind if he can't keep up with us!'

Uncertain what had suddenly galvanised Percy into such urgent action, but sensing that it meant danger for Esther, Jack ran after them, then skidded to a halt in the side alley alongside the bookshop just in time to see the two constables kick in the door at the foot of the stairs. By the time he got inside the premises at the head of the stairs, he could see clearly through the office door. One constable was pinning a man's head down on a desk, while another had a woman's arms up her back as she knelt, head bent forward, on the carpet. Percy was holding Esther to his chest as she cried hysterically. Jack rushed in, and Percy stepped aside as he invited him to comfort Esther. 'She's had rather a traumatic time,' he said.

'To put it mildly,' Esther choked as she turned her tear-streaked face towards Jack.

'Are you harmed?' he asked, his heart in his mouth.

'It's nothing that a stiff brandy won't cure,' she managed. 'Then we can begin packing ahead of our move to Watford.'

'What was the significance of that name?' Jack asked as he and Percy sat in a commandeered office inside Bow Street Police Station, while in a room down the hall Esther was being examined by a hastily summoned police surgeon who'd already given her a mug of tea containing a sedative.

'Spencer Mallory? For once your memory for names almost failed you, you idiot!'

'Never mind the name-calling,' Jack replied angrily. 'I remembered in the end, so get off your high horse and explain. I'm a senior Scotland Yard officer, which you're not — not anymore, anyway — so *tell* me!'

'Sorry, Jack — it must be the shock, followed by the need to rescue Esther. Spencer Mallory was behind all those murders in Bethnal Green three years ago. Indirectly, anyway, and you once rode on the back of his coach to follow his wife to a meeting with her lover.'

'I remember that much at least,' Jack confirmed, 'but that was all about that niece of our upstairs neighbour who'd gone missing. No wonder I didn't associate the name with your simultaneous enquiries into the Bethnal Green murders.'

'Quite right,' Percy conceded. 'You weren't really involved in the investigations into the Bethnal Green murders that Mallory was behind. He was once a solicitor, and the leading light behind a company known as Gregory Properties that bought up large tracts of housing in Bethnal Green when it was learned, from information supplied by a fellow director who was on the LCC Planning Department, that they were planning to knock down the houses and erect a new housing scheme.'

'Ah, yes — now I remember that his name came up in one of the files I received,' said Jack. 'I think civic corruption was the charge?'

'Much more than that, since his company hired Mangler Maguire — or "Michael Truegood", as he was calling himself — to terrify or murder the tenants who refused to leave their homes. But we never managed to stick Mallory with anything other than fraud and corruption, for which he served two years,' Percy replied. 'That's no doubt why he wanted his revenge against me. I assume that he went into contract catering when he'd served his time, and came out unable to practise as a solicitor anymore. What purports to be the governing body of all solicitors claims the right to ban the blatantly bad ones from practising. It all makes sense now.'

'I still can't work out how he's connected to the death of Thomas Benton.'

'We can acquire more information on that connection from his widow — the woman calling herself "Cora Bligh". We'll interview her in the morning.'

'Not today?'

'No, for two good reasons. The first is that you need to escort Esther home in the coach that I've already ordered, and make sure that she rests for as long as it takes for that sedative to wear off. Secondly, it's been my experience that suspects speak more honestly after a night in the cells staring at bare brick walls and fighting off the rats.'

'You said that you'd seen Cora somewhere before — aside from at your farewell party?' said Jack. 'Do you remember where?'

'Yes, it's just come to me,' Percy replied with satisfaction. 'She was a receptionist at Mallory's old solicitor firm, so perhaps she was more involved in the Bethnal Green murders than we originally thought. Anyway, I think your wife's ready to go home,' he added as a figure loomed in the doorway.

'She is indeed,' Dr Baines confirmed as he looked down at Jack. 'The sedative was only a mild one, but even so she'll need to take to her bed when you get her home. If she shows signs of sleeping in tomorrow morning, you should let her. She's physically unharmed, you'll be delighted to learn, but the ordeal would have been most stressful, and she may experience nightmares for the next few weeks.'

'Thank you, Doctor,' Jack said as he rose to leave, then turned back to Percy. 'If I'm missing tomorrow, you'll know why. But before I leave, I'll give instructions for Cora Bligh to be held overnight, and we can interview her the next time I'm in.'

'We can't hold her for too long without charging her,' Percy reminded him, 'so why don't I interrogate her in the morning, if you're not here?'

'One very good reason is that you're no longer on the force. The other is that I want the pleasure of doing so, given that she was one of those holding Esther against her will.'

'How are you feeling now?' Jack asked Esther an hour later, as the coach rattled along the road out of Plaistow and towards Barking.

Esther leaned against his shoulder as she replied sleepily, 'Very tired, but a good night's sleep will take care of that, according to the doctor.'

'I'll look after the children at breakfast,' Jack promised, 'so that you can get a lie-in. Was it *so* bad?'

'That awful woman was all set to carve my face up if I didn't answer their questions,' she recalled. 'I'm afraid I told them everything in order to avoid that knife.'

'That doesn't matter, since we have them both in custody now. If I know Percy, he'll suggest that we offer Cora a deal to peach on Mallory.'

'But surely you're in charge now that Percy's off the force?'

'A good point. I'll remind Percy of that in the morning. And I'll see that Cora gets charged with threatening you with a knife.'

'Don't do that just on my account,' Esther replied. 'Right now, I think I'll just close my eyes and snooze on your shoulder. But I'm not so tired that I've forgotten our bargain.'

'Me neither,' Jack replied as he kissed the top of her head. 'Tomorrow I'll look up the railway timetables for the services between Watford and Euston.'

CHAPTER SIXTEEN

'I trust you had an uncomfortable night?' Percy gloated as he and Jack sat across the table from Cora Bligh the following afternoon. By prior agreement, Percy was leading the interrogation. They were hoping that no-one in Bow Street recalled, or had ever known, that Percy was no longer a police officer.

When their prisoner maintained a sullen silence, Jack decided to prod her a little harder. 'Why did you threaten to carve up my wife's face?' he asked coldly.

'Your wife, was she?' Cora replied. 'I admire her taste. I always did go for handsome rozzers.'

'Like your late husband, Thomas Benton?' Percy asked. 'If you thought so highly of him, why did you have him murdered?'

'What do *you* know about these things, Granddad?' Cora demanded bitterly.

'Tell *me*, then,' Jack offered, sensing that she was about to open up.

She sighed, and they saw tears welling in her eyes, despite the dim lighting in the interview room.

'Four years ago, I had everything,' she recalled sadly. 'A handsome husband who seemed to think the world of me, a pleasant and secure job working for a successful solicitors' firm in the Strand, and every prospect of a happy future. Then Thomas did the dirty on me.'

'He was a copper, just like me, wasn't he?' Jack asked encouragingly.

'That's right. One of the best, they reckoned. Not one of those head-kickers employed down the East End to chuck drunks out of pubs, but a real gent, whose duties included guarding the nation's politicians in Parliament, and lining the Mall when the Queen was parading down it. He even met the Queen, once.'

'So did I,' Jack replied, hoping to increase the intimacy to a level at which she might be more forthcoming. 'She gave me a bravery medal.'

'Your wife must be very proud of you,' Cora said weakly.

'What went wrong?' Jack asked gently, although he knew the answer.

'I wasn't enough for him, was I?' she replied, allowing a tear to roll down her face. 'He started molesting women he was supposed to be taking into custody — those "Votes for Women" types. Anyway, he got caught and drummed out of the police, and we were struggling financially. I couldn't bear him touching me, after what he'd done, so he started spending what little money I was bringing in on prostitutes, down in the Docks area.'

'But you were still keeping the money coming in, with your work in the solicitor's office?'

'Yes,' she replied with a twist to her mouth. 'Then I made a big mistake — I fell in love with my boss.'

'Mr Mallory?' Jack asked quietly.

Cora nodded. 'It began innocently enough. I could see that he was very depressed, and one day I plucked up enough courage to admit that Thomas and myself were having difficulties, and that was why I'd been guilty of one or two minor errors in my work. He said he'd overlook them, since he knew what it was like to have a marriage come apart. He went so far as to reveal that his wife had been carrying on with his business partner, and that the twins born to her, which he'd always thought of as his, were in fact the result of her affair. We were like two lost souls, and we began an affair of our own. Nothing sordid, you understand — just two unhappy people seeking comfort and reassurance.'

Several more tears rolled down Cora's cheeks, and Jack reached into his jacket and handed her a clean handkerchief.

'Why should you be interested in all this?' she asked.

'Because I know how I'd feel if my wife were unfaithful to me,' Jack replied, while Percy remained tight-lipped and silent. 'How did the affair progress?'

This provoked a bitter chuckle. 'Spencer played me good and proper. Once we were on intimate terms, he revealed that he had business interests in the East End — Bethnal Green, to be precise — and that he needed someone he could trust to send or carry messages down there to a man called Michael Truegood, regarding tenants who were unwilling to move from their hovels. I had no idea they were to be murdered, honestly I didn't, but once the truth emerged I was terrified that I'd somehow be implicated. But Spencer promised me that I wouldn't, then offered to marry me once he'd divorced his wife. Imagine how I felt — the prospect of a new husband, a man at the top of a wealthy profession. Then he went to gaol, thanks to *you*!' She glared at Percy, who remained silent.

'You waited for him to serve his sentence?' Jack asked.

'Yes, more fool me,' Cora replied as she dabbed furiously at her eyes. 'For two bloody years I waited for that rat. Then when he came out, his wife had started divorce proceedings anyway, and it seemed that all that stood in our way was Thomas, to whom I was still married, although I'd moved out of the rooms we'd shared in Vauxhall. I was living in a very smart house in Aldwych, which Spencer paid for.'

It fell silent, and Jack decided to push his luck. 'But you didn't divorce Thomas, did you? He was murdered in Bethnal Green, wasn't he?'

'You obviously know about that, and I'll admit to organising it, even though it was Spencer's idea,' Cora said with a sigh. 'Looking back on it, I think it was all part of his plan to have me so heavily implicated in his crimes that there was no going back. Never trust a smooth talker who appears to be able to offer you just what your heart craves. Look where it's landed me, with nothing left to look forward to except a horrible drop from some scaffold somewhere.'

There was no stopping the tears now, and she spoke between choking sobs. Then Cora took a deep breath and pulled herself together, clearly determined to tell the whole story. 'We pretended that Spencer had some work lined up for Thomas, acting as a bodyguard for a few prostitutes he was running in Bethnal Green, and that the job was his for the asking if he agreed to a divorce. Spencer wasn't a pimp, of course, since by then he'd started the catering business, but Thomas didn't know that. A job associating closely with prostitutes obviously appealed to him, so he agreed to accompany me to meet the man in charge down there. He was a man called George Mulherron, and when I led Thomas to the prearranged spot in a back lane leading off Brick Lane, Mulherron came out of a dark doorway and smacked him with a hammer. We ran away as fast as we could, but almost collided with a copper coming the other way.'

'What made you go back for the gold watch?' Jack asked.

'Greed, among other things,' Cora admitted. 'But Spencer also persuaded me that it would be good to get it back, once I'd told him that Thomas's name was in it. We were hoping that his murder would look just like all the others, you see. But as luck would have it, the copper who was there when I went to collect it recognised me from the night we passed him, running away from Thomas's body. So I panicked and gave him the watch to keep for himself, and arranged for Spencer to silence him with a bribe. That must have been about the time that Spencer dropped the pretence, and just started using me like a cheap prostitute, threatening to go to the coppers if I didn't do whatever was asked of me.'

'And by then you couldn't just walk away?' Jack suggested.

Cora nodded and looked at him pleadingly. 'I really *wouldn't* have cut your wife's beautiful face, honestly I wouldn't. But Spencer was determined to get the truth out of her, and thank God she realised that he meant it. She told us how you'd sent her in there to get evidence that Strand Enterprises had been behind the attempt to poison old Granddad here. Except I picked the wrong beer glass, and some other senior copper got it.'

'Did Spencer say why he wanted you to poison Detective Inspector Enright?'

'He never stopped raving on about it from the first moment we got the circular that went to all the outside catering concerns in the centre of London. Spencer recognised the name and blamed him —' she nodded towards Percy — 'for the fact that he got banged up for two years. I wasn't keen on doing the deed, believe me, but by then, as I said, Spencer held so much over me that I was scared to disobey him. Perhaps I should have cut my losses after Thomas was murdered and just run away. But, you know, a woman alone in London doesn't have much option but to sell her body, does she?'

'Some do. My wife took in sewing, until we met,' Jack replied quietly.

Cora suddenly reached out and grabbed his hand. 'I wish to God I'd met you instead of Thomas Benton. Like I said, I always had a thing for handsome coppers, and you're so — well, so *nice* as well, I suppose. We could have had a wonderful life together, but just because I let my impulsive heart rule my head, I've finished up here, and I'll end my life kicking on the end of a rope. Oh, dear God!'

Cora rested her head on her arms and began to sob. Jack was too embarrassed to know what to say or do, and looked across at Percy, who gestured with a jerk of his head that they should make a discreet exit.

'We'll come back when you're more composed,' he told Cora on their way out.

'I don't know about you,' Percy muttered once the door was closed and they were back in the corridor, 'but I could do with a mug of tea.'

'First of all,' Percy said to Jack as they locked eyes over two steaming mugs in the basement canteen, 'I want to congratulate you on the finest piece of interrogation I've ever witnessed. And that's not just idle flattery — you've really come on a long way.'

'I had a good teacher,' Jack replied as he blushed slightly, 'but that wasn't a show on my part, nor was it a stunt. I genuinely feel sorry for the woman.'

'Nothing to do with her good looks, or the way she was making up to you like you were God's gift?' Percy asked with a smirk. 'That type are the worst — they hope that with a little flattery you'll go easy on them. I'm a little disappointed that you fell for it.'

'I didn't fall for anything,' Jack insisted. 'She was genuine, and she's had a hard trot for the past few years. Do you have *no* compassion left in you?'

'Of course I do, even though she called me "Granddad",' Percy said. 'But she *was* intending to cut Esther's face to shreds.'

'I don't believe she'd have done that, even if Esther had remained silent,' Jack argued, 'although thank God she didn't. And Esther said not to charge her with that just on her account.'

'That's perhaps as well,' Percy said, 'since I intend to go back in there and offer her a deal.'

'I *knew* it!' Jack replied, greatly relieved.

'Well, think about it for a moment — what evidence have we got against Mallory without her testimony? We could obviously send her to the drop in Newgate based on what she's told us already, but Mallory would simply wring his hands in despair, then pretend to be innocent of the murders he's arranged. Our only way of making sure that Mallory hangs is with Cora's testimony. And if she performs in the witness box the way she did half an hour ago, then he's a goner.'

'So what's the deal you have in mind?'

'Cora walks free of all charges, in exchange for her agreement to testify against Mallory.'

'How do you propose to bury all the crimes she's just admitted to?'

'Watch and learn from the old dog, my boy — he still knows a dodge or two. Have you finished that tea?'

Back in the interview room, Cora Bligh had composed herself, and now sat rigidly upright, clutching the handkerchief that Jack had given her earlier.

'Do you still want this back, with my snot all over it?' she asked sheepishly.

Jack shook his head. He and Percy took a seat, and Jack left it to his uncle to take the lead.

'Chief Inspector Enright and I have been considering the sad tale you told us,' Percy told her, 'and it seems to me that it's open to other interpretations.'

'Enright?' Cora echoed. 'So he *is* your granddad after all?' she asked Jack, who shook his head.

'He's my uncle,' he told her. 'And a very wise man who it would be in your best interests to listen to very carefully.'

She remained silent as Percy continued.

'One could well understand, after the humiliation you suffered when your late husband was dismissed from the force, how you might have been persuaded, by a very sympathetic employer, to become his mistress in return for financial security and a warm feeling of being both valued and needed. But you also felt some lingering compassion for your disgraced husband. So when Mr Mallory offered to find a new job for the man you intended to divorce, you grasped the opportunity, totally unaware that Mallory wished to have a potential rival for your affections taken off the playing field. You innocently took Benton down to a supposed meeting with a future employer, then suffered the trauma of watching him being battered to death. You ran from the scene, half believing that you would be next, and failed to notice that there was a local constable coming the other way. Then, when you found yourself in financial trouble, you were tempted to reclaim the gold watch that you knew Thomas had been carrying.'

'You forget that I offered it to that rozzer as a bribe to keep my name out of it, and that my lover at the time gave him another sweetener,' Cora reminded him.

'You offered him the gold watch when you realised, to your horror, that you were suspected of complicity in your husband's murder because of the fact that you were seen running from the scene. You had no idea that your employer had given the man another bribe to keep silent about the entire business. And I can categorically assure you that the constable who took those bribes is in no position to admit to it.'

'And the poisoning?' she asked.

'You were of course employed as the supervisor of the catering at my retirement function,' Percy continued. 'Mr Mallory told you that he wanted to get his own back on me for my part in putting him away for two years. He ordered you to put a substance in my beer that would make me feel light-headed by the time I came to make a speech, which in the event I never did. And, of course, you got the wrong beer glass anyway. But you only ever intended to play a mild practical joke on me, and had no idea that what you dropped into the beer glass was deadly.'

'You should be writing books, like Mr Dickens or Mr Hardy,' Cora said. 'But that's a rather different story from what I told you earlier, which was the truth.'

'I know that, you know that, and my nephew knows that. But any jury called upon to assess the guilt of Mr Mallory will only hear the version I just gave you.'

'You want me to send Spencer Mallory to the gallows?'

'Wouldn't he do the same to you, if the roles were reversed?'

'Probably. But what about my threat to cut the face of that lovely wife of yours?' she asked Jack.

'Since you never went through with it, I don't think she'd want to proceed with any charge against you. I think she'd feel sorry for you, because *she* got me, and you didn't.'

'Cheeky bugger,' Cora said with a chuckle, then transferred her gaze to Percy. 'So I'll walk away, free of any charges?'

'If you agree to peach on Mallory in front of a jury, certainly,' Percy confirmed.

She reached out and gripped his hand. 'I'm sorry I called you "Granddad".'

'I'm not,' Percy said, 'since I'm childless, and you're probably the only one who ever will.'

CHAPTER SEVENTEEN

'I suppose this will be the last family Sunday lunch gathering for the foreseeable future,' Percy said gloomily as he smothered his roast pork with apple sauce.

'You'll all be very welcome to come to the new house in Watford once we get settled in, if it's not too much of an effort to travel up there,' Jack replied.

'Your uncle would travel to the North Pole for a free lunch,' Beattie reassured him.

'He may not have to,' Lucy said, 'since Teddy and I intend to keep up the tradition once we move into my old family home here. The Bunting Lane house is as good as sold to a lovely elderly couple who're keen to move out of Paddington.' She turned to Esther. 'Will Polly and Alice be moving with you to Watford? Only we'd like to bring Billy and Nell with us when we move down here.'

'Yes, I'm delighted to say,' Esther replied. 'The new house has a staff cottage in the rear garden, and when we all went to inspect the property they expressed their delight at having their own place. Polly has family in Hemel Hempstead, which isn't all that far from Watford, and Alice has an admirer who works in Epping, which is the same distance from Watford as it is from here, except in the other direction.'

'What do you make of the new house, Jack?' Teddy asked.

Jack smiled. 'You'd probably approve, being an architect. It's at the entrance to a huge private estate, and was built some forty years ago. It's a very solid, red-brick construction in what I'm told is called the Queen Anne style, with several turret rooms at the top, which the children will no doubt convert into fairytale castles or Roman fortresses in due course.'

'It's just across the road from where I'll be working,' Esther added, 'and the children will be able to play in the estate grounds on warm days. Although it's privately owned, the public are allowed to picnic there on public holidays and weekends.'

'You must be very excited to get your very own school,' Lucy enthused.

'It's not exactly *my* school, since it's privately owned,' said Esther. 'But I'm looking forward to teaching again.'

'She got through a month's course in just one week,' Jack interjected proudly, 'and her teacher was so impressed that she invited her to become her deputy in this new school.'

'It's actually quite an old school,' Esther corrected him. 'It's been in existence for the past twenty years or so, but has fallen into decline, with the enrolments diminishing. There are only twelve or so pupils left, and none of them are aged over ten. We're hoping to extend into classes for pupils aged up to fourteen, or even older. If we can improve the quality of the education they're receiving, we might be able to persuade the parents of the existing pupils to let them stay on for another four or more years. My first task will be to improve the educational levels of the existing classes, and of course I've had experience with children of that age from here in Barking.'

'I suppose that these privately run schools, that charge fees, are superior to the one here in Barking?' Teddy asked. 'Jamie and Clarissa attend the Board School closest to us, in Gray's Inn Road, but I'm not overly impressed with the education they seem to be receiving. There's a private school not far away in Highgate, but they charge very high fees.'

'I can't really comment on the differences between Board Schools and private ones, obviously,' Esther admitted, 'but one has to assume that since private school teachers are paid more than the others, they can attract the best.'

'Like you,' Jack said proudly.

'How did Esther persuade you to move away from here anyway?' Teddy persisted as he looked across the table at Jack. 'Leaving the old family home, and all that. I'm surprised you agreed — I'm not sure I would have done.'

'Let's just say that I'm very fortunate to have one of those rare husbands who are prepared to concede that their wives can contribute to society,' Esther replied as she leaned closer to Jack and planted a kiss on his cheek.

'And let's just say that she saw her opportunity and struck a bargain with him,' Percy muttered as he reached for another pork slice before Beattie could stop him.

'And nearly got my face rearranged in the process,' Esther said with a shudder.

'Cora claimed that she had no intention of carving you up,' Jack replied, 'and so far as I can tell, she was telling the truth.'

'Did I miss something exciting?' Lucy asked.

'You remember that woman working as the assistant for Strand Enterprises, who obligingly gave you a quote for a make-believe function — a Miss Bligh?' said Jack.

'Of course. I've never been so glad to get out of a place,' Lucy replied with a grimace. 'And by the way, that "make-believe function" recently became a *real* one. It's sometime next month, and you're all invited. We're not employing Strand Enterprises, obviously.'

'Well,' Percy added, 'when you refused to go back there, to ask why the quote you got was much higher than the one for my farewell do, Esther volunteered, in exchange for Jack agreeing to move to Watford.'

'Sorry, Jack,' Lucy muttered.

'It wasn't that simple,' Jack explained. 'The deal was that I'd only discuss the possibility in exchange for Esther making the enquiry, but that it would become what the French call a *fait accompli* if she needed rescuing from danger. Which, as it turned out, she did.'

'That Miss Bligh produced a knife,' Esther put in, 'while her employer tied me to a chair and threatened to have my face cut open if I didn't reveal why I was really there. Which, unsurprisingly, I did, so we'll never know if she would have carved me up like she threatened to do.'

'She claimed to have only carried the knife for her own protection,' Jack added, 'and who can blame her, moving in the murderous circles that Fate left her with no option but to mix with?'

'You're showing a lot of sympathy for someone who could have reduced my face to raw meat,' Esther protested, and Beattie pushed her unfinished plate of away with an expression of disgust. 'Sorry, Aunt Beattie,' Esther added, 'but I really *did* earn my move to Watford the hard way.'

'And Cora agreed to peach on her boss — a man called Spencer Mallory, with whom I had unfinished business from a few years ago, during all those murders in Bethnal Green,' Percy explained. 'When he learned that he was being invited to cater for my retirement do, he saw his chance to poison me, but Cora chose the wrong glass to drop the cyanide into.'

'*I* wouldn't have missed,' Beattie grunted, 'and now that even Percy has finally conceded that he's retired, I'll have more opportunities to poison him myself. For the time being, he's proving very useful around the house, although I've seen better wallpapering. Jack's old room looks as if it was re-papered by one of those new French artists — suggestions of images here and there, none of them quite aligned with each other.'

'It was *your* choice of wallpaper,' Percy reminded her, 'and I redeemed myself when I repainted the outside privy, did I not?'

'If you like brown privies,' Beattie conceded. '*Quite* the wrong colour to have chosen.'

'Well, I'm glad he's retired, anyway,' Jack said, chuckling. 'I can now concentrate on doing the job I'm paid for.'

'Before you return to recruiting more young men to a life of underpaid and undervalued servitude, keeping the haves safe from the have-nots,' Percy said to Jack, 'when does Mallory come to trial?'

'Sometime next month, according to the Newgate calendar,' Jack replied. 'Cora Bligh seems to have been as good as her word up until now, and we'll definitely have him for poisoning Montague, although I'm not so sure about tying him to the Bethnal Green murders.'

'That doesn't necessarily matter,' said Percy, 'since you can only hang once, and the appeal court routinely knocks back clemency appeals from poisoners. Bear that in mind, Beattie.'

'This conversation has gone in *quite* the wrong direction,' Beattie protested, 'so let's get back to Esther's new career, shall we?'

Jack watched from the doorway as the covered wagon rumbled away from the front door of the Church Lane house on its first trip to Watford, carrying almost all the heavy furniture. Esther stood behind him, stopping the children from racing after it.

'Bertie wants to know when he'll get to ride in the wagon,' she told Jack after kissing the back of his neck.

'How many more times does he have to be told?' Jack said with a tut. 'We'll all be in the back of it for the final trip, which, if we're lucky, will be by nightfall. I'm glad we sent Polly and Alice ahead to prepare things for our arrival, so at least we'll have something to eat on our first night in Watford.'

'You're getting as bad as your Uncle Percy,' said Esther. 'I can only hope that now that you're free of his dreadful influence, you'll not be returning home so full of food.'

'Yes, I imagine that it's back to cheese sandwiches and leftover meat pie. Does your new school do meals, by the way?'

'Healthy lunches, certainly,' she replied, 'so I don't think you'd be interested. And thank you again for agreeing to the move.'

'I very foolishly entered into a bargain with a beautiful lady of my acquaintance, which I lost,' Jack replied, then his face became more serious. 'Thank God no harm came to you. I swear I'll never expose you to anything like that ever again.'

'I've heard that before,' Esther scoffed, 'but perhaps there's a greater chance of my not being used as bait in some criminal investigation now that you're no longer involved in active duties, and your uncle has finally retired. Although, being Percy, he even managed to turn *that* into a big drama.'

A NOTE TO THE READER

Dear Reader,

I hope you were as delighted as I was to be invited back into the lives of the Enrights as they make the transition from the dying days of Victoria's long reign into that decadent decade that historians call the Edwardian era. England was changing rapidly, and so are the Enrights, in their own way.

Most notably, the relationship between Jack and his Uncle Percy has evolved somewhat. When we first met them, as they combined their efforts to identify and bring to justice the infamous Jack the Ripper, Jack Enright was a naive, inexperienced police constable pounding the beat on his first posting in Whitechapel, while Percy was already a veteran of service in the Metropolitan Police, and one of the elite Scotland Yard detectives. He was also Jack's life mentor, following the years in which Jack had lodged with Percy and Aunt Beattie in Hackney, and had been so fascinated by what he heard of Percy's life in the police force that he followed him into it.

During their joint investigations, covered in the eight previous novels in the series, Jack always looked to Percy to take the lead, and Percy grew comfortable with always having Jack at his elbow, never questioning his authority, both as an uncle and as a higher ranking 'bobby'. But in this novel we can clearly see a changing of the guard; not only did Jack finish up at a higher rank than Percy in the Met, but by the end of their final, official joint investigation, he is the *only* police officer in the family, and no longer prepared to be talked down to. Percy has finally retired, and Jack must make his future career progression on his own.

But that is nothing compared with the momentous change in Esther's life. When we first met her, she was Esther Jacobs, an orphan living alone in a grubby Spitalfields tenement and earning her living as a seamstress. She is now Esther Enright, mother of four and a middle-class housewife living in the old Enright family home in Barking. She has just discovered a latent talent for teaching that was no doubt honed in the upbringing of her four offspring, and with the encouragement of her own mentor she's about to launch herself into the world of education. And what a transitioning world it was.

Until the middle years of Victoria's reign, education was a haphazard business. The only schools that existed were those either sponsored by various Church denominations or established by charitable founders who called them 'free grammar schools', except that they were not 'free' in a financial sense. The result was a largely illiterate, innumerate workforce that didn't fit the nation's ambition to lead the world in commerce and manufacturing, and several Acts of Parliament were passed in order to ensure that even the 'common' folk had the essentials that England required of its citizens. From 1870 onwards, education was compulsory for children aged from five to ten years of age, although some parents still put their children to work in the fields or the factories.

The raising of the school leaving age to eleven in 1893 — four years before Esther entered the system officially — had no effect on attendance levels, and Attendance Officers proved ineffective in ensuring that school enrolments matched the size of the local infant population, particularly since parents were obliged to pay a nominal fee for their children's education, and even though they were breaking the law if they kept their children away from school. Not until 1891 did education become genuinely free.

Along with the attempt to make what we now call 'primary' education compulsory came a system under which control of the quality of that education was devolved to local 'school boards' of the type encountered by Esther. In the belief that quality of teaching could somehow be guaranteed by requiring would-be teachers to be trained for it, the authorities insisted that entry into the teaching profession be limited to those who had gone through a prescribed, unimaginative, training course. Trainees were also required to complete a prescribed period in front of a class, under supervision by someone who had been through the system ahead of them.

It was little wonder that under this typically Victorian straightjacket of rules and regulations those charged with the task of filling curious minds with learning did so with boring stolidity. Classroom discipline was stern and often brutal, and learning was 'rote fashion', rarely rising above the copying of what the teacher had chalked on the blackboard onto scratchy slates, because paper was too expensive. And even I can remember, in my early schooldays, parroting my 'times tables', and being physically punished if I made a mistake.

Teachers were often uninspired, barely educated beyond the level required in order to pass it on to their pupils, and only in it for the meagre wage that they earned. Little wonder that the vast majority of teachers in those days were single women existing on a pittance, because men could earn more even as labourers, while married women had children to look after.

This explains why Esther seemed like a breath of fresh air to Emily Allsop — a rarity that came along only once in a generation. She was comfortably middle-class and well educated herself, she wasn't in it for the money, she knew all about children, and she had already learned for herself that being a successful teacher involved actually engaging the interest of those who were learning, and that education for life required more than the so-called 'three Rs' of reading, writing and [a]rithmetic.

So dire was the public education to which the average child was exposed that parents with ambitions for their offspring were prepared to pay for it, and in late Victorian England 'private' education was big business. But like any business, success depended upon the delivery of a quality product, and when Emily Allsop invited Esther to join her in her new fee-paying enterprise, she was feathering her own nest at the same time as fulfilling Esther's ambition.

With Jack and Esther's immediate future secured, what of Uncle Percy? Will his lively, inquisitive brain be fully engaged in cultivating vegetables in a garden which, as he admitted to Jack, is only a means of escape from house arrest under the demanding gaze of his wife Beatrice? A clue to the answer to that question can be found in the pages you have just read. We have by no means heard the last of Percy Enright, nor will his nephew Jack be free of his 'assistance' in the novels to come.

If the references to the murders in Bethnal Green seemed vaguely familiar, or if you'd like to learn about how Percy brought them to an end, then you should read *The Slum Reaper*, book four in this series.

As ever, I would be delighted to see a review of my book posted on **Amazon** or **Goodreads**. Alternatively, feel free to visit, and contact me on, my author website: **davidfieldauthor.com**.

Happy reading!

David

Sapere Books is an exciting new publisher of brilliant fiction and popular history.

To find out more about our latest releases and our monthly bargain books visit our website:
saperebooks.com

www.ingramcontent.com/pod-product-compliance
Lightning Source LLC
Chambersburg PA
CBHW020909180626
46816CB00007BA/2314